Witch of the White Serpent

Witch of the White Serpent

DAWN OF THE BLOOD WITCH BOOK 4

Maria DeVivo

4 Horsemen
Publications, Inc.

Witch of the White Serpent
Dawn of the Blood Witch Book 4
Copyright © 2023 Maria DeVivo. All rights reserved.

4 Horsemen
Publications, Inc.

4 Horsemen Publications, Inc.
1497 Main St. Suite 169
Dunedin, FL 34698
4horsemenpublications.com
info@4horsemenpublications.com

Cover by J. Kotick
Typeset by Autumn Skye
Edited by Laura Mita

Library of Congress Control Number: 2023932940

Paperback ISBN-13: 978-1-64450-888-6
Hardcover ISBN-13: 978-1-64450-885-5
Audiobook ISBN-13: 978-1-64450-889-3
Ebook ISBN-13: 978-1-64450-890-9

Dedication:

For Babaysh—You make all this worth it. You are my always.

For Lil' Cat—For always supporting me and my craziness, and for loving Modir the way you did.

For Morgs—It's always for you, and always will be for you … just maybe when you're much older.

Table of Contents

Chapter One. 1
Chapter Two 14
Chapter Three 29
Chapter Four 42
Chapter Five. 52
Chapter Six. 70
Chapter Seven 85
Chapter Eight. 99
Chapter Nine 112
Chapter Ten 125
Chapter Eleven 139
Chapter Twelve 154
Chapter Thirteen. 166
Chapter Fourteen 179
Chapter Fifteen 192
Chapter Sixteen. 203
Chapter Seventeen 215
Chapter Eighteen. 227
Book Club Questions 243
Author Bio 245

Chapter One

In the Time of Darkness
In the Age of Ice
Wintertime, 666 AD
The Frostheim Forest of the Far Northlands
Night of the Full Moon

Every time a gust of wind blows, packed snow from the treetops drifts quietly down from above. The night is clear—no cloud in sight to produce the white flakes of winter. Snow descends from the arms of the trees when the wind makes them do their wiggly dance to and fro. The light of the full moon and the scores of twinkling stars fill the forest with a reflective white light bouncing up from the snow on the ground giving the clearing the illusion of day-light. I've brushed away a swath of snow and with a large stick, drew a circle with the star in the center of it, and Aizel, my beautiful, red-haired companion, placed the rune stones at every point of the star. Now, the torches are lit, and the heat from them makes this frigid night somewhat bearable, but the longer we stay out here waiting,

1

the more irritated Aizel and I both become. We need Sorcia so we can get on with the ritual.

If there's one thing I absolutely detest, it's waiting … in the cold. And if there's one thing I detest more than waiting in the cold, it's performing a love spell.

So, here I stand … in the cold, waiting to do a love spell.

Come to think of it, I really do hate participating in love spells. They never turn out the way the sorcerer intends; there are too many unintended consequences in the aftermath, and they're messy. I know better than to have agreed to do this. I'm smarter than this. Better than this. *So why are you here?* I ask with my agitated, inside voice. Why do we do anything, really? Maybe for the slightest chance that something will turn out differently…

Standing at the northernmost point of the star, I clasp my hands together and blow into the little space between to warm them up. To my right, Aizel looks at me with a sideways glance and mimics my action.

"Are you sure you told her where to meet us?" I raise my voice above the howl of the rushing wind.

"Blodwyn," Aizel huffs, "Sorcia knows our spot. It hasn't changed since we were ten years old. She'll be here." She's annoyed too, but she's better at hiding it than I am.

Chapter One

I fidget in place, trying to keep my legs from freezing. "I know, I know," I say with an aggravated voice. "You know how much I…"

"…hate waiting in the cold," she finishes for me with an eyeroll.

I smile at her. Under the moonlight, under the sky littered with stars, and against the orange glow of our torches, Aizel is a pure vision—my oldest friend, my faithful companion, my covenmate; she complements my every whim and desire with temperance and patience, and she calms my burning rage with peace and serenity. Yet she indulges me in whatever experiment or spell I wish to concoct, and together, we have brewed the most delicious and malicious work this side of the Frostheim River. If not for Aizel, I don't know what trouble my quick temper and curiosity would have gotten me into.

I swiftly run my hands up and down the sides of my long-sleeved cloak to try to generate some heat in the upper part of my body.

"Blodwyn," she huffs again, "you can't be serious! It's not that cold out here. Quit exaggerating. You're bothered because…"

"I hate doing love spells," I blurt.

"You hate doing love spells," she repeats matter-of-factly.

"Are you sure you told her the right hour? Are you sure you said Owl Hour and not Raven Hour?"

"Yes, Blodwyn!"

"If it's the hare she's having trouble getting, I could have gotten the cursed thing myself!"

"You and I both know that this is Sorcia's request. This is Sorcia's spell. She needs to be the one to make the sacrifice."

I nod. "Yes, but why? How many times have we done exactly this to no avail? She should know better!"

We *should know better*.

"True. But you know how desire works. And right now, Sorcia's desire lies in Grom. We can't ever know the whys or reasons behind it, but..."

Grom was my partner once. Our brief relationship ended before the passion had a chance to come to fruition. When my mother found out we were experimenting with coupling, she cut the courtship down. I can't blame her; I was nearly thirteen, and he was three years my senior. And while my lingering feelings of love and desire for Grom had died out over the years, I had often found myself wondering—if I had been a little older, or if it had been a different place or time, would we have lasted? I had often dreamed of his long blond hair draped over my stomach as he inched his tongue to my nether region. And I often remembered the time when my mother inadvertently entered my chamber while he was doing such things to me, which ultimately led to her dismissing him from our home. Dreams. Memories. Call them what you will. That was long in the past. Yet still—hearing of Sorcia's budding relationship with him had sent a twinge of jealousy into my heart and stirred up some of those old dreams and memories that had been dormant for five years.

"Grom is not for her. I know this," I spit out.

Aizel cocks one of her thin eyebrows up in a perfect arch. "Oh, and how do you know this? Please tell me you don't still have feelings for him."

I shoot back a similar glance. "Don't be crazy! That was ages ago. I was but a child when he was in my life. If that's who Sorcia now wants to be with, I have no reason to protest."

Aizel glares at me suspiciously, and the wind picks up again causing my long white hair to dance wildly around my head. The noise of the gust fills my ears and steals my breath from my throat with its invisible icy fingers.

That's it! I've had enough. I extend my arms out at my sides to create a temporary energy barrier around us in the circle. Instantly, the wind ceases to howl, and we are both enclosed in the warmth of my shield. Aizel sighs with relief and lowers her head in thanks.

"This won't last long," I say. "Hopefully until she gets here."

Aizel closes her eyes and breathes in deeply through her nose, filling her lungs with the calm air inside my forcefield. She smiles, and I suspect she's thankful for the ease at which the air enters her nostrils without the gripping sting of the open elements. I want to reach across the circle and grab her hands and dance happily with her under the pale moonlight, but before I can let the thought fill me further, Sorcia comes bounding through the trees. Her tan leather boots crunch the snow underfoot, and I lower my arms, breaking my barrier and allowing Sorcia entrance into the circle. Her doeskin cloak shows speckles of dark brown, and she drops a bloodied linen package into the center of the star before taking her position to my left.

The bundle comes undone at its center fold revealing the body of the dead, white hare. Only it's so soaked with its own blood, its fur is tinged pink. "Apologies, sisters," she says out of breath.

"The heart?" I inquire with a raised brow.

"Yes, yes," she assures and procures a second bundle from under her cloak. "I wanted to keep it safe."

Aizel chuckles.

I don't. I motion my hand in front of me, signaling for Sorcia to lead in the spell. She nods, and Aizel clears her throat to alert me she's centered and ready to begin.

Sorcia unravels the heart of the hare, reaches over to the torch closest to her, and burns the fabric. The acrid smell of the bloody cloth consumed by the flames fills the space around us, and I breathe it in so as to become one with the smell. It washes over me, through me, and seems to lift my feet a fragment off the ground. I grow uneasy, for I sense a shift in the air that is unfamiliar to me. It puts me on high alert.

Sorcia cups the heart in both of her hands and raises her arms in front of her. Against the moonlight, the heart looks black. Inky. Still dripping with its dark red blood. I close my eyes and see it beating still. And through the smoke of the torches and the smoke from our breath on this cold night, I see Sorcia using her hot blade to slice through the fur and muscle and bone of the creature. The flesh of the thing sizzled and smoked in the cold night, and Sorcia plunged her bare hands into its chest cavity to attain the still-beating jewel. But that happened hours ago, yet it's happening now in the fog, through the smoke. I see both events converge before my eyes—the images bleeding together, becoming one, yet remaining separate. It's hard for me to discern the here and the now. The nowhere. These things I see, from moments past—moments of the immediate past, moments that I should have no knowledge of, but somehow, right now, I do. I open my eyes and look around, disoriented. The ritual has barely begun, and already, I'm feeling the breadth and depth of some powerful force, some powerful entity, like godly, watchful eyes seeing through my own.

Aizel crinkles her nose at me, but I don't acknowledge the questioning gesture.

"Accept this offering of the hare," Sorcia chants, holding the heart above her head. "I make this sacrifice to the old ones so they can bless me, your loyal servant, with love and an abundance of fertility."

She lowers the heart to her mouth and rubs the organ's dark red blood across her lips. But it's not red. It's black in the darkness. Her tongue darts wildly over the flesh of the heart—meat and veins, and chunks—and the inner workings of the organ are like a trail in the snow across her face.

And the heart is still beating...

Aizel chants in our foreign tongue—the language taught to us by my mother. I hear her singing and humming words of praise and glory, but to my ears, it is merely in the background. For coming from the deep of night, from the depths of the forest, a new sound emerges. I can't tell if it is there in the wild or coming from inside my head, but there's another song—pulsating through me, getting louder and more pronounced with every second that passes.

"My ancient brethren! I beseech thee. Hear my prayer. I call upon you to bless me with the desire of my chosen one." Sorcia places the heart in the center of the circle, next to the carcass of the hare. She reaches for the dead animal and pulls from it a handful of blood-soaked hair. It's long and straight and white like mine. Turning to the torch, she throws the hair into the flame. "The one called Grom," she says. "He is whom I truly desire." The hair singes with a hiss and lets off a foul smell.

Yet, the invading song continues. It grows in my chest and in my head—an almost deafening dirge of unfamiliar voices, yet I've heard them all before in my dreams. They sing to me. For me. And I struggle to hear the words of their song, to make out the urgency of their message, so much that I scarcely notice as Sorcia opens her cloak, removes the knife from her belt, pulls her long, black braid of hair over her shoulder, and saws it off with her blade.

A gesture never performed in this ritual.

Aizel gasps in shock, and I remain motionless, still distracted by the unseen movements from the depths of the wood, the song of the ancients rushing in my head, and a deep growling voice speaking to me in the pit of my chest with a guttural sound that makes my insides churn. Sorcia's eyes dance with the firelight of the torches, and the runestones adorning the edge of the circle glow orange. Aizel looks to me sharply as worry and confusion wash over her face.

Sorcia holds her severed braid up to the sky, throws her head back, and in the ancient tongue of the old ones screams, "I summon thee to bind my desires—to bind my heart to the heart of Grom, to join my flesh to the flesh of Grom, to tether my soul to the soul of Grom."

Before I can protest, she swivels her body around and puts the thick braid of her severed hair to the fire, twirls it around herself three times, then tosses it on top of the carcass in the circle. The bloody bundle ignites and a furious wave of burnt hair and fur and singed linen permeates the space around us.

"Sorcia! Wait!" Aizel cautions.

But it is too late. The blade is already against Sorcia's palm. She squeezes her fist against the cold metal and lets the thin line of red drip into the fire. Something in the forest screams—a high-pitched wail that stings my ears. By the timbre of it, I can tell it's neither human nor animal. Sorcia laughs triumphantly and sways her body to and fro—drunk on the smells of her offering, drunk on her own confidence.

Aizel falls to her knees in despair, the blood drained from her face, and the look of pure terror glowing in her blue eyes. "What have you done?" she whispers in desperation. "What have you done?"

Sorcia stops her dance and stares at her. "What do you mean? I completed the spell. It is done. Grom will be mine. The old ones accepted my offering."

They didn't, a voice growls, startling me.

I try to say something. I want to protest and give my opinion on the events that transpired, but when I open my mouth to speak, nothing comes out. When I try to move my legs forward, I can't. I'm paralyzed. Stuck. I can turn my head to look around me in all directions, but I have no mobility in my arms or legs. Sorcia and Aizel argue over the spell, and I physically cannot contribute to the debate. It's like I'm not even here in the circle. It's like I'm looking at them from beyond the circle—above the circle.

Because I am.

Their words are just noise echoing in the background of my head. The real voice speaks loudly now—the voice from the woods, the voice from the sky, the voice that has stretched out through space and time. Sharp jagged rock scraping across cavern walls. It grates on me yet soothes me at once. It is like warm honey in my throat, or a summer rain on my naked flesh, or Grom's face between my legs, and… I blink, and the images of Sorcia and Aizel fade in and out, like they are disappearing from this reality. But maybe it's me who's really disappearing? Shifting. Transcending. I'm here, but I'm not. A strange light shines down and around me. I throw my head back and look to the sky. Adjacent to the moon, a cluster of stars has gathered and has formed what appears to be a rip in the darkness. A tear, a gash, an opening, a hole that's vibrating and pulsating and *singing* to me. Its music is beautiful—a cacophony of discordant sounds and instruments yet unknown to man. It is the song of time—of time long ago, of time now, and of time yet to come joined in marriage and entangled in each passionate note and tone.

Oh, Aizel! Oh, Sorcia! Can you hear it too? I think to myself.

They are gone, the voice replies. *They are not in this place with you.*

Suddenly, I am afraid. I am afraid that I am not alone. The voice is unfamiliar and unnerving.

Be not afraid, it says. *I go before you, always.*

The hairs on my arms stand straight up, and I am overcome with *knowing*. The one who speaks to me isn't one at all. It *is* all. It is all and everything punching through the vastness of the world—the collective voice of my kin and the old ones, of the now and the here, of the nowhere. I look to the rip in the sky again and from behind it, a red light tries to filter through. Like it's trying to worm its way through the gash of the opening. The heat from it fills me and makes me smile. I want to be one with it. I want to be one with the song and the voice and the old ones, for I see the vision of it. It's so clear to me now. The teachings of my mother fall into place, and I finally see! I finally see through that opening, through that hole—the old ones roam and rule on the other side of the cosmos with their monstrous forms and gnarled limbs—like giant, twisted trees struck by lightning. And their mouths are the beaks of crows, and the mouths of snakes with forked tongues licking up the flames left in their wake. The sky is stained red with the blood of the people who were deemed unworthy to exist in their world while those who were saved live freely in this utopia with power unmatched and uncontested. It is the dawning of the time of the heksas with the Blood Witch to guide them. The red light urges itself to be born, to punch through the space and time, to flood itself into my world and swallow me up.

And a thought invades my mind, taking my attention away from the opening:

The Blood Witch.
The Blodheksa.
My mother.
Modir.
Modir is alone in our cave.

Icy dread works its way into my veins, and I blink rapidly again. The vision of the sky fades, the red light fades, the images of the old ones fade, and all are replaced with Aizel and Sorcia in the circle in the throes of a heated argument.

"Blodwyn! You know why I had to do it," Sorcia whines with hands on hips.

I shake my head back and forth as my body works itself back into feeling. "Something's wrong," I mutter.

"Exactly!" Aizel exclaims. "Tell her how dangerous that was!"

"Something's wrong!" I say louder.

Aizel approaches and puts a hand on my shoulder. "What do you mean?"

"Modir. Something's wrong with Modir."

Sorcia *tsks* her tongue against the roof of her mouth. "You were just with her a few hours ago. She was fine then, right?"

Aizel rolls her eyes and ignores Sorcia's question. "Blodwyn, how do you know this?" Aizel asks gently.

"We need to go back now. The old ones told me."

Chapter Two

In the Time of Darkness
In the Age of Ice
Wintertime, 666 AD
Caverns in the Far North
Night of the Waning Gibbous Moon

The stench of death permeates the air around me. It's subtle, barely noticeable, and as much as I don't want to acknowledge its presence, I can't deny it's there. Rancid undertones of decayed flesh hit the back of my throat with each breath I take in through my nose or my opened mouth. It practically gags me—makes me choke on the horrid aroma. But I'd rather choke on the smell than the sadness that swells inside my heart. It's hard to swallow the hard lump in my throat when I'm trying not to breathe in the stinking smell of death.

My mother's death.

Modir's legs stretch out in a "v" on the cold, rock floor of our cave, and I prop the heavy bear-skin blanket to help support her back and relieve some of the pressure on the lower half of her body. For three days now, she has twisted and turned in agony, and she howls like a she-wolf at consistent intervals. I try my best to make her feel comfortable and comforted, but I know there really isn't much I can do except to make sure she drinks her water, keep her as warm as possible, and stroke her hair from her face.

Because she's dying.

At a moment when all should be right and good, at a time that is normally a happy one for families, the woman who has been my guide, my protector, my teacher, and my confidante for all my seventeen years of life is dying.

She's dying so she can bring my brother into this world.

Aizel is our village's unofficial midwife. She brings over a bucket of warm water, dips a linen rag into it, and wipes Mother's nether region in hopes of gently coaxing the child out. When she takes the cloth away from between her legs, it's saturated in bright red blood. Aizel gives me a sorrowful sideways glance. I've seen her perform miracles with the births of some of the villagers' babies, but this time, I'm not confident there's one to be had.

Modir grasps my hand tightly as the spasms in her womb rock her senses. The flesh on her distended stomach is taut against the shape of the child within, and the deep purple stretch marks that race up and down the entire circumference of her belly seem to grow wide and then collapse with each movement of the babe—like claw marks made from an ancient cloven-hoofed demon.

Modir loosens her grip on me when the contraction passes, and she sinks back into the bolster holding her up. Aizel looks at me again, the same concerned glare of helplessness glowing in her eyes. She nods her head curtly, and we rise from the floor to speak privately at the altar in the corner of the cave. Sorcia cleanses the birthing tools, and a torrent of anxiety overcomes her when we approach the sacred area.

"Is… is… is she? Has she? The baby?" she stutters uncontrollably.

"She's dying," I say, matter-of-factly. "The moment the child decided to be born was the moment she began the process of death."

Aizel lowers her head, unable to meet my gaze straight on. "Yes," she whispers as if telling me a secret. "I'm afraid so, Blodwyn." Her voice catches in her throat with a small hiccup sound.

"No!" Sorcia gasps.

"Does she know she's dying?" I ask.

A faraway look invades Aizel's eyes. "I can't tell. I think she has some notion." She pauses, takes in a deep breath, then says, "Blodwyn? Has she ever mentioned if her labor with you was difficult?"

I shake my head. "She never spoke of such things. Why? Do you think there's a way to save her?"

"Oh, please, Aizel!" Sorcia cries with a whispered tone. "You have to! You must!"

Aizel lowers her head more. Her deep red locks cascade over her face hiding her eyes from me. "No. She just needs to live long enough for the baby to arrive. And then..." her voice trails. "I can make her a tincture to ease the pain. And there's a spell to..."

"No," I interrupt. "No magic. Mother was clear about that."

"But, Blodwyn," she pleads, "she's been suffering for three nights now. The words of the Bkär draugrs would..."

"Speak not the names of the ancients in her presence!" I snap coldly.

"I'm sorry, Blodwyn. You're right," she relents.

"Are you sure you can't save her?" I say, and my voice bounces off the cave walls and back to my head with a deafening echo of desperation.

Aizel doesn't respond.

"But why? Why now? Why like this?" Sorcia pleads. The desperation has affected her voice as well.

Aizel shuffles her deerskin boot against the rock. "I think the baby was in there for too long. Whether she held him inside for all those years willingly or whether he chose to stay inside is beyond me, but something kept him in her belly for seventeen years. Seventeen years, Blodwyn! The sheer nature of the amount of time alone is disturbing. You were meant to be twins— the duality of power, yet something prevented his birth."

A cold wind blows in from the opening of the cave and the torches in the main atrium sputter and flicker. Mother cries out against the noisy blast, and the three of us quickly go back to her side. Aizel inspects Mother's opening again and continues to wipe away the excess blood from between her legs while Sorcia assists her. I go back to my place to hold her hand and comfort her.

"Blodwyn!" Mother calls for me.

"I'm here, Modir. I'm here," I coax, petting the side of her face. She's burning up. A line of sweat beads form at the crown of her forehead, and I motion for Aizel to pass me one of the rags.

"It sounds like *Fimbulvetr* has begun out there," Mother says breathlessly.

"Oh no," I say jokingly. "The long winter has not begun! I won't let the gods start their Ragnarok on the day of my brother's birth!"

She smiles. It's weak and closed-eyed. Her facial movements are languid and dreamy like she's in some kind of in-between state. Now and here. Nowhere. "You could defy the gods if you wanted to, my dear," she whispers with a low and grumbly voice, like a snake rattle shaking in her throat. "You possess a power like no other."

"Speaking of the gods, Modir, please let Aizel give you something for the pain, or at least to calm your nerves."

Her eyes bulge from their sockets with wild fury. "No. I told you, absolutely not. I will not have magic interfere with…" Her voice trails with another ear-splitting scream from another contraction. This one closer than the others.

Aizel sets herself on the balls of her feet and bends Mother's knees up. "I'm going to need you to push hard very soon but only when I say so. Only when I say," she instructs.

Mother nods. "Blodwyn," she mutters. "Blodwyn, come closer to me."

I lean in just enough so her lips brush against my ear, and I try to hold my breath to prevent the death smell from invading my senses.

"Blodwyn, my sweet daughter. *You* are the Blodheksa. It will be you. This I know."

Sorcia eyes me sharply with a look of surprise. I know these words were supposed to be only for my ears, and by the look on her face, it is apparent that Sorcia is not very pleased with what she overheard. "Mother! Stop right now. *You* are the Blood Witch for you have brought me, the Blood Sister, into the world, and now you bring forth the Blood Brother on this night. He will be here soon enough."

"No, no," she moans, as the beginning of yet another contraction shows plainly on her face. "There must always be the three. And you were an aberration, never meant to be the Blodsøster. The gods have plans for you. That's why they kept your brother in my belly all these years, so *you* could grow and develop and mature in your abilities on your own. It is you. My Blood Witch. You will drench the world in the blood of the people."

"But what of the babe? What of the boy?" I ask desperately.

"You must take care of him, Blodwyn. Your brother, Trond. He is special. He is necessary. You will need him as he will need you."

She knows she's dying. She's aware of her organs shutting down as the hands of death stroke her from the inside. Hot tears spring to my eyes and blur my vision. Up close, her visage appears cracked and jagged through the watery pools, but I can't be sure if that's how she looks to me now or if that's how she's looked since forever. "Don't talk like that, Modir," I cry. "You're not going anywhere."

"You know the only thing keeping me alive is Trond. I think he's kept me alive for many, many years. Once he is born..."

"Stop it! Silence!" I scream, and another rush of wind shrieks through the cave. "I don't know how to take care of a child! What will I do?"

Mother gives a small smile of approval. "Temper, temper brings the tempest," she sings. "You'll be fine, Blodwyn. Just keep your good thoughts flowing. You'll raise him so you will be prepared for when it is your time to bring forth the Blodsøster and the Blodbrødre."

Her little rhymes always calmed me down, even from an early age. If I had ruined a ritual or had trouble exorcising a draugr from a villager, I would often get blinded with rage at myself for my own failures and shortcomings. But Modir knew how to ease my anger. She had trained many a witch in our village, and she always had taught that every witch, every heksa, had their own set of skills that could be mastered. We were all different, and with practice, time, and patience, we could open the gateway to let our ancestors, the old ones, back into the world.

"But you are the best," she whispers, reading my mind. "You were always the best. And that is why it will be you."

I pull back a little to look at her. She looks serene. At peace. A blush of pink rises in her pale cheeks, and her eyes dim from their normal icy blue to a deep shade of a midnight sky. She no longer squirms with labor pains. "He's coming, isn't he?" I ask, but it's not really a question.

Mother's face contorts, and she squeezes my arm with whatever energy she has left. Aizel hadn't given her the signal to push, but Modir already knew. It was time.

"Yes! Yes! That's it!" Aizel coaches.

Mother grunts and pants and squeals with pain, but there's a smile in her eyes that tells me it's alright. That it's going to be alright.

But it's not alright.

I am scared to think of a life without her—it frightens me to the core. I am scared to death of the child remitted to my guardianship—it is something I never asked for. Or wanted. Because deep down, I don't have the heart to protest. Deep down, I don't have the fortitude to defy my mother. The truth of the matter is—*I do not want to be the Blodheksa.*

"There you go! There you go!" Aizel shouts over the screams of the wind.

"I love you, Blodwyn," Mother says dreamily to me, but not *directly* to me. "I love you, Trond," she calls out in her strongest voice. She bears down and screeches as she forces out one last push. Her body relaxes as the baby is expelled from her womb.

"He's here! He's here!" Aizel cries, and Sorcia whizzes around in a blur with the garments and water and items needed to aid her. I look down to Mother's widened legs. There, in Aizel's arms, is a bloody mess of a child with wrinkly, pale skin, and a shock of bright pink hair. Quickly, they get to work to remove the cord, clean him up, and clear his airways.

"He's pink!" I exclaim. "Why is he pink?" A sudden rush of fear grips me. "And why isn't he crying?" I ask frantically. "Aizel? Shouldn't he be crying?"

"Relax, Blodwyn. He's just fine. There's just a lot of blood and..." She swats the baby on his backside, and a wave of relief and joy comes over me when he gurgles and lets out a hysterical, bleating wail.

Tears of happiness slide down my cheeks. "Modir!" I say at her shoulder. "Modir! He's pink! He has a head of bright pink hair! He's Ruz!"

"And he's perfect!" Sorcia chimes in as she helps wrap the child in linen.

But there is no movement from Mother. Her back slightly arched against the bearskin, her eyes closed, and her head slumped to the side. I nudge her shoulder, and her body flops a little in a subtle way, in a lifeless way. Because that's what she is now—lifeless.

"Modir?" I squeak, but the knot in my throat forms fast and hard. "Modir?" I repeat, my brain not fully coming to terms with the events unfolding before me—the shrieks of new life from the corner at the altar bouncing off the cave walls mixed with the silence of death in the middle of the open area. I shake her shoulder, harder this time, and my voice rises a frantic octave. "Modir!" I press my body against the side of hers and descend into a fit of despondent hysterics.

She's still so warm.

Aizel and Sorcia ignore me. They leave me to my emotions as they tend to the baby. *Trond*: my new brother who is now solely in my care. My mind races with a flood of anxiety and questions and doubts and...

Anger.

So much anger I can't see straight. Between my tears and my rage, the world looks jagged again. So jagged that I could tear open the sky with just a mere glance and open the gateway to let the old ones flood in and destroy the earth. Mother's body is so warm against mine, and I pull her close against me absorbing what is left of her spirit—the scent of her sweat-tinged skin, the perfume of her long, red hair, the metallic smell of her blood spilled on the granite floor, even the way death smelled when it first descended upon

23

her three days ago—all of it! I absorb it all at once in my nostrils and mouth. I hover my hands over her chest and create a white light-orb to suck back into me whatever is left lingering of her soul on this plane. I pull her in, drink her in, fill myself with the last mortal remnants of her essence so she'll be with me forever.

I breathe in deep and hard yet find it difficult to catch my breath. I choke on the panic in my chest and pant and gulp for air.

"Blodwyn," Aizel says in a stern voice from across the room. "Blodwyn, breathe. Through your nose, out your mouth." She's worried; it's obvious. I don't blame her either. With the child in her arms, she won't be able to subdue me if my rage gets too out of control.

I do as she instructs and settle my breathing down. I close my palm, and the white light of Modir's last piece of energy shoots up my forearm like lightning piercing the ground. It burns as it races through my veins, and I shudder from the shock of it. It travels up to my shoulder, singeing the fine white hairs on my arm, leaving behind the odor of burnt flesh. Modir's body goes completely limp and topples over, but I'm too enraptured with what her lifeforce has left behind in me—on me.

Quickly, I remove my cloak and roll up the sleeves of my shirt. Black etchings appear on the entirety of my right arm—from the bones that jut out on my wrist up to the curve of my shoulder. The runes of the old ones manifest themself on me, in me. They tell the story of the great Blodheksa who never was. The one who hid the boy inside for seventeen years and passed her power to her daughter. It's the story of Mother. I read it out loud with a strong voice, in the language of the ancients, and Trond suddenly stops crying.

Aizel gasps, hands the child to Sorcia, and rushes to me. "What are you saying? What did you do?"

I lift my right arm in the air for her to inspect, and her eyes go wide with wonder.

"Tha… that's remarkable!" she gushes with confusion. "How did… when did…" she stutters, but I ignore her half questions and train my eyes on the child in Sorcia's arms.

She sees me staring and saunters over to me. Trond is wrapped in a dark brown blanket, his little pale body safe and secure and swaddled. All I can see is his shock of white hair still stained pink with his birthing blood, and I secretly wish for it to never be washed away. I secretly wish that he will stay pink forever so as to remind me of Modir's ultimate sacrifice.

"I pray he's as special as she said he is," I mutter.

Aizel gives a small smile. "She named you the Blodheksa, didn't she? It's written there on your arm." She twists and turns my arm in every which direction. "You pulled the last of her essence into you?" she exclaims. "How did…"

"Aye."

Sorcia kneels next to me. "You really did it, Blodwyn! We only heard about the possibility of that ritual, but…"

"I didn't perform a ritual, though," I interrupt.

"But you did *something*!" she beams. "You accepted, did you not? To be the Blodheksa?" Her dark eyes flash with gold for a split second, and I stiffen. I know she heard Mother speak the words, and Sorcia's question leaves me a little uneasy.

"Aye," I answer with a small voice, and Trond starts to wriggle and fuss.

"Take him. He's yours," she says, handing him to me.

I hesitate. I've never held a newborn before, and I'm still not sure of how I feel toward him. I'm confused, and in awe, and happy, and sad, and scared, and angry… so, so very angry… My eyes drift away to some far-off daydream of red skies and burning trees, and my arm with the new etchings starts to tingle and get hot. "He's not mine," I growl.

"It's fine, Blodwyn," Aizel encourages. "It'll only be for a short while. Then you'll be his."

I don't understand what she means, and I don't have a moment to inquire for Sorcia wastes no time in plopping the bundle in my arms.

He coos and settles in the crook of my arm and looks up at me with an enormous set of stormy gray eyes. They flash with lightning-like flickers—like the white-light orb of Modir's soul creating the rune carvings up my arm. She's still telling her story through us, her beloveds. And I can't help but smile because some of the last remnants of Modir are in him too. She has stayed with us, even if it's just small pieces of her.

"Hello, there, Ruz," I say playfully in a high-pitched voice. "I promised our mother I would take care of you, so that is what I intend to do."

He wiggles again and opens his mouth with an animal-like caw.

"About that..." Aizel says, and the timbre of her voice gives me reason to pause.

I raise my eyebrows.

"He's going to need to eat soon."

"And..." I question.

She hesitates. "Well, Blodwyn, he'll need to feed. From a mother."

I swivel my head to Modir's lifeless body on the floor behind me, and tears rise again in my eyes.

"Just for the first time," she assures. "Then I can get a new mother from the village to act as a substitute."

My mind goes blank. I hadn't thought of feeding Trond or how I would keep him alive if Mother were to die. "I... I can't... can you do it, Aizel? When he needs to drink from her, please. I can't do it."

She nods. "Of course. Then we'll prepare her for the pyre."

"Pyre?" I screech, and Trond jolts in my arms. "No. No pyre. I'm burying her, Aizel."

Sorcia puts a hand on my knee. "Blodwyn, you know we can't bury her."

"I don't care what the village council says! I don't care what the people say! I don't care about whatever tradition we're supposed to abide by! Modir will not be put on the pyre! I am not burning my mother!"

Chapter Three

In the Time of Darkness
In the Age of Ice
Wintertime, 666 AD
Caverns in the Far North
Afternoon of the Waning Gibbous Moon

Aizel had Trond suckle once from Modir then quickly took him to our village to find someone who could support his needs. Even though she is the youngest midwife at seventeen years old, she is certainly the most trusted and skilled. There is no doubt in my mind Aizel will find a suitable wetnurse for my brother. There is also no doubt in my mind that she wanted to leave our cave as quickly as possible. I know Modir's decaying body in the wide-open space of our living quarters was too much for her to bear. Plus, I don't think she knows how to react to my declaration of a burial, so leaving with an important quest was the only reasonable option for her. Modir was a second mother to Aizel, and her passing must be hard for her, too. Aizel was only nine when her own mother died, and

Modir took Aizel into our family with loving and open arms. We were raised as sisters along with other children who came and went throughout the years.

While Aizel went off with the baby, I sent Sorcia to the west village to enlist the assistance of her lover, Grom. My history with him and his deep care for Modir alone should propel him into action and bring him to my place in the forest. He is the only other person I trust to help us dig a grave for Mother under the concealment of night. Maybe trust is too strong of a word, though. It's more like he is the only person I know who would keep that knowledge a secret as a tribute to the woman who treated him with such kindness at a vulnerable time in his life. When I told Sorcia of the plan, she eyed me coldly, which I ignored. The brown in her eyes flashed green with a spark of jealousy and resentment for a split second. The "yes" sounded sour when it rolled off her tongue— sour at the fact that we couldn't finish her love spell. Is she worried that Grom and I might reconnect on some level? I hope that's not what she thinks. I have no interest in him or anyone else for that matter. All I'm interested in right now, at this very moment, is burying my mother. Getting her cold body in the cold earth where she will be safe and sound.

Until I can bring her back to life and she can retake her rightful place as the Blodheksa.

I stroke her red hair away from her face as I cradle her head in my lap. She's gray, ashen, the life clearly drained from her body. And yet, I feel her still. My mind wrestles with her physical absence and her spiritual presence. How can she be here, but not? How can I feel her but not hear her? How can I see her but not *see* her? Her shell remains, unanimated, stolen by death, yet she lives through me, in me, and on me in the runes tattooed upon my arm. Every thought of her makes the carvings pulse and etch deeper into my skin like needles driving into the layers of my flesh. I'll surely go mad if I keep these thoughts in my mind, for such a good person on earth should not have been ripped away and apart as she had been.

Her whole life, she had cherished being a mother. And maybe it was her position as the Blodheksa that made her embrace that role completely. See, Modir was like a mother to many children in the village, often caring for those who had lost their fathers and mothers in raids or from sickness. Our home was a revolving door for the less fortunate and needy, and Modir was a champion of the downtrodden. My own father had died shortly after I was born, and my mother had vowed to never know another man. With Trond still resting in her womb, she knew she would bear no more until he arrived, so she became somewhat of a foster mother. She was warm, and kind, and funny, and loving, and welcoming, and all children loved her. There was an innocence in her that rang true to the souls of the children, making them kindred spirits.

The people in the village called her The Great Healer for she knew potions and brews and tinctures that could bring down fevers and cure diseases. She knew all kinds of spells to mend cuts and bruises and even broken limbs, but the best of her medicine was in her spirit that she bestowed onto others that uplifted their souls. Those on the borderline of suicide often sought her counsel for she would take them on spirit walks—trances that would walk them through the depths of their *hugrs* and *fylgjas*, the deepest parts of their cores, and quell their depression. The blood of the old ones ran hot in Modir's veins, imbuing her with power so massive and intense, I don't think the people in the village would have been able to fathom her true intentions.

Modir hid well in plain sight.

She couldn't hide from me, though, and she can't hide from me now.

My tears fall onto her gray cheek, and the steady stream of hot, salty water seems to sizzle against her cold face. She is cold. So very cold. But I piled the blankets on top of her and built the fire in the room dangerously high to try to help her warm. It suffocates me—makes me sweat and want to tear my own clothes off, yet underneath the mound of animal skins, the weight of her lifelessness radiates through. The frozen weight of her death permeates through with its icy grip—a savage reminder that she is gone, gone, gone.

"Blodwyn?" a voice calls from the mouth of the cave. I close my eyes and sense the presence pass over the threshold. "Blodwyn? Aizel? Are you here?" Sorcia's deep voice snaps me from my despondent thoughts and stiffens my back at attention. I anticipate the burly growl from Grom to follow her into the cave.

But it doesn't.

It's just Sorcia.

I rapidly blink my eyes as she comes closer into focus.

"Oh, sweet Blodwyn," she sings in a high-pitched tone. "You've been here with her all this time."

I ignore her sentiments. "Where's Grom? Is he out in the forest? Did he start digging already?"

Her shoulders slump forward, and her ebony hair falls over her downcast eyes. I cringe at the sight of it so short. "He... he said he's not coming, Blodwyn," she says, defeated. "He said he doesn't think he can help us."

"What? Why?" I raise my voice in disbelief and the markings on my arm pulse hot against my flesh.

"He said he doesn't believe it's the right thing to do. He said he believes she would have wanted a traditional cremation and..."

I shimmy my body from under the dead weight of my mother and jump up to meet Sorcia face to face. "You agree with him, don't you," I accuse. "You think we should put her to the flames!"

Sorcia shifts in place, bouncing her hip from one leg to the other. "I... I don't know," she whines. "I can see both sides to it."

"Or is it because you don't want me to be in Grom's debt?" I snap.

"No!" she snaps back. "Why would you think that?" Her button nose scrunches into a ball at the center of her face.

"Because you're jealous!"

She gasps, "Blodwyn!"

"Oh, forget it!" I yell and wave my hands dismissively in the air.

"I am not jealous!" she asserts, stamping a brown leather boot on the pavement.

"I said to forget it."

She sighs, which is her way of shifting the topic. "Grom says he has much respect for your mother. He says that what she did for him as a boy made him the man he is today."

I chuckle sarcastically. "She took him in as an orphan, Sorcia. And when she found out he took her only daughter's maidenhead at twelve years old, she made him leave."

Sorcia shudders at my words. The reality of my relationship with her now lover hits her deep in her chest.

"Of course, he *had* to become a man," I continue. "He had no other choice. But she still cared for him. Kept watch over him. Made sure he was well and not starving or alone. The least he could do for her is to put her in the ground!"

"But he will not defy the Village Council. The Jarl of Frostheim would…"

"I don't care about the Council. I don't care about the Jarl. I don't care about their made-up rules. We will wrap up a stag and set it on the longboat. No one will be the wiser. In the meantime, Modir must be buried. And if Grom won't help me," I grit my teeth and speak in a low and threatening growl, "I swear by the old ones, misfortune will rain down upon him for a century's time." My arm twinges again. It burns. A whiff of burnt flesh rises to my nostrils, and I look down at the etchings. The white, unmarked patches of my skin blaze with a hot pink hue. I breathe in deeply to try to settle myself down.

Sorcia takes a step toward me and places her hand in mine. "I loved her too; you know that right?" Tears spring to her eyes.

"Of course," I croak against my sadness. I had almost forgotten that Sorcia was in mourning as well.

"Maybe Grom is right, though. Maybe we should just do the right thing."

I yank my hand from hers and angrily swat away my tears as if they were a thousand annoying flies hovering around my eyes. "Right? How dare you speak to me of what is right? If we put her on the pyre, she'll be gone forever. But if she's in the ground, I will do anything and everything in my power to bring her back. Bring her back so she could be the Blodheksa and fulfill everything she ever spoke about—everything she ever taught us about."

A shocked expression invades her face. "Blodwyn... I heard her say it. I heard her tell you that you're the Blodheksa now."

"No, Sorcia. I'm the Blodsøster. I've always been the Sister. My whole life, that's all I've ever known. That's all I've aspired to be."

"So, what? You plan to bring her back? To life? But if yours is the power to be wielded, then wouldn't that, by definition, anoint you as the Blodheksa, making your mother's existence null? If you could perform such a miraculous feat, then..."

"Words! Words! Words!" I scream, and my voice densely fills the cave. Sorcia places her hands over her ears to block the deafening sound. "Stop your words! Your spells! Your suppositions! If I must dig into the ground with my bare hands, I will!"

A strong wind blows in, and I can't quite tell if it's the actual air that makes the fire and torches flicker, or if it's the manifestation of my anger in the space between Sorcia and me. She takes a step away from me, and a look of fear washes over her face for a split second. Sorcia has always been afraid of me to some degree although she would never admit it. Fear and jealousy. Fear because she was never certain as to what the full extent of my abilities were, and jealousy because I lived the life she had always dreamed about—most importantly, she had wished my mother was her own. Sorcia was no orphan and needed not my mother's love and attention in that respect. She had lived in the outer village with her family of the nomadic tribes (as was evidenced by her dark hair and eyes) and was always silently considered an outsider when she was around us.

"I don't think that's going to be necessary," Aizel says, entering the cave with baby Trond wrapped tightly in her arms and two figures peering over each of her shoulders.

My shoulders relax, and I sigh a sigh of relief at her arrival. "Aizel!" I exclaim. I rush over to her and scoop Trond into my embrace. Only his face is visible through the bundle, yet he smells of honey and all things sweet. He coos and wriggles at the sound of my voice. "Hello there, Brother," I sing sweetly. "I missed you so." I plant what seems like a hundred kisses upon his soft forehead and nuzzle the strands of his white hair that peek through at the top with my nose.

The woman behind Aizel also carries a child in her arms—another neat little package bound in linen. With her free hand, she pinches her nose and scrunches her face tight, and that's when I realize there's an offensive odor coming from the body. I guess I had been in here too long to notice it, but at the woman's physical reaction, it was apparent Mother had begun to turn.

"This is Arik and Ylfa," Aizel says, leading them into our home.

"And our daughter, Halli," the woman pipes in.

Aizel gives me a strange look before continuing. "Arik, Ylfa. This is Blodwyn and Sorcia."

We all nod at each other with customary pleasantries.

"I knew your mother," Ylfa blurts. "My mother is an apothecary in the village, and your mother would come by often. They would talk and share many a tale. I would bring them tea during their chats and sit with them sometimes. She was always so sweet and so kind. Never a bad thing to be said. My mother is devastated to hear of her passing. Anything we can do to help you would be our pleasure."

"Ylfa's babe was but three months, Blodwyn," Aizel says. "I delivered sweet Halli myself, but sadly she is no longer with us."

Ylfa rocks the bundle in her hands lovingly, and I soon come to realize it's nothing but a wad of cloth wrapped up to look like a baby within. "The cold took her," Ylfa says nervously. "But we hope she'll be back soon." She smiles heartily, and it unsettles me.

"Ylfa has agreed to nurse Trond for us," Aizel continues. "I've examined her, and there is still sustenance from her breast. I promise she is a good match. Strong."

I nod, but I know Aizel can sense my hesitation. *She's not one of us,* I say to Aizel's mind. *If she nurses Trond, he will darken her. Damage her. Her sanity will fade in no time.*

Aizel raises an eyebrow. *Does she look like she's sane now?* she responds.

I give a small shrug. "They'll have to stay here," I say in a hushed voice.

"Yes. Yes, of course," Aizel assures. "That matter has been settled already."

I look to Ylfa and bow my head in thanks. She's a stocky young woman with ashy blonde hair set in a high bun atop her head. Her rosy cheeks are so pink, they're almost red, and it's not just from the chill of the winter's bite. There's blood rushing throughout her whole body—the blood of life. The blood of a healthy new mother whose instincts have shifted into high gear. The blood of a fierce warrior woman bent on the survival of her young, even when her young was no more. She will make a fine wetnurse indeed. Trond will feed furiously from her breast, making him strong and capable. In my mind's eye, I envision her breasts—the skin of them hot pink like her cheeks look right now, engorged and practically overflowing with her mother's milk, the nipples throbbing and begging to be relieved of the pressure within. As if on cue, Trond squirms again and furrows his platinum brow. He must have read my mind for a tiny hunger roar escapes his mouth.

Ylfa's eyes widen, and she scurries to take him from me. "Look at that!" she gushes. "Little man is hungry again!"

I turn my attention to Ylfa's mate, Arik, and I eye him up and down. He's a hulking specimen of a man who towers over me like a monolith rising from the horizon. His long orange braids flow over his shoulders and down the middle of his waist. He looks like a warrior—an authentic *rekkr*, but if that is true, then why does he stand in the middle of my cave with his wife and not on the battlefield? I move closer to get a better look at his countenance, and that's when I see the thick scar racing diagonally across his face from the side of his forehead across his closed, sunken-in eyelid, over the bridge of his nose, and cutting a line right through his bushy orange beard. His right eye is cloudy, like a fog has settled there. I suspect he is blind, or nearly so.

Ylfa notices me inspecting her husband and shuffles in her place nervously. "Blodwyn," she speaks up, "your reputation precedes you. Your mother spoke very highly of you and the things you can do. Yes, it is an honor to nurse the child for you, but I do ask of something in return."

"Oh?"

"Arik will help you bury your mother, and we swear by the gods of all time that we will not reveal this to anyone. We will take this to our own pyres. But, please, all we ask is that if there is anything you can do to restore Arik's sight. He completely lost the one in battle, but the other... disease has robbed him of his vision. I want him to be able to look upon the face of the beautiful life we create! We would be forever in your debt. Seven times over."

I put my hand on Ylfa's shoulder and nod. "I will do my best."

Chapter Three

Sorcia comes forward, takes her by the elbow, and guides her to the back alcove. "Come with me, Ylfa. I'll show you where you will stay," and they hurry off to the back halls.

I step closer to Arik to inspect his countenance better. In this proximity, he can see me, or parts of me, or shadows of me—I'm not sure exactly how much, but he sees something because I jerk my head at him—at his face, at his scar. "Raid?" I ask.

"Aye," his voice rumbles. It reverberates deep in my chest through my thick layers of clothing, and I immediately get the sense that he is a man of few words.

"And your enemies?"

"Dead."

I nod in approval.

Arik lifts his head to the ceiling and breathes in through his nose, inhaling the foul stench of decay from the body in the room. "Modir?" he asks.

"Aye," I respond.

"Forest?" he asks.

"As soon as possible."

Chapter Four

In the Time of Darkness
In the Age of Ice
Wintertime, 666 AD
The Frostheim Forest of the Far Northlands
Night of the Waning Gibbous Moon

A rik lifted Modir's heavy body and flung it across his shoulders. Closely, he followed me to the hallowed spot of the Frostheim Forest — the place where Mother had taught me so many things about the world, and the past, and our lineage, and our power. I had picked a spot close to her favorite trees, and Arik wasted no time clearing away the snow and ice as he pierced the ground with his tools. He was silent the entire trek over, which was for the best. The silence allowed me time to wander in my thoughts and recharge some of my energy. Now, Arik grunts with each movement, each heave and ho of his spade. It's the thick shoulder bone from a wild beast that he uses to dig into the packed earth and scoop the dirt into a massive mound.

Being outside in the frigid air always seems to replenish my soul—the core of my power. But I'm not cold. I know I should be. I know I should be annoyed by the bite in the air. I should be irritated by the wind stealing my breath. But I feel them not. In fact, with my bottom on the ground, and my back against the oak, I could easily disrobe to my undergarments, and I don't think I would even feel the cold. Or could feel it, for that matter. My branded arm sends waves of pulsating warmth throughout my entire body.

"You were marked," Arik says holding the spade high above his head.

I shuffle uneasily in my spot. "How do you know? You can't see it," I say, defensively.

"You don't deny it," he answers and continues to dig.

"What do you know of runes?" I ask after a few uncomfortable moments.

He stops and wipes the sweat from his brow. "I know the power. Charms. Spells. My own mother was a *seidr*," he answers, his words come out in short, choppy sentences. Barely sentences.

"How can that be? Seidrs are dark and solitary—most without families or inner circles. They worship the serpent gods. They are not of my ilk."

He ignores my comments and continues, "Serpent gods, sky gods, old gods, they're all the same. My mother was marked. Like you. When I was a child—when I had my vision, I saw her brands. But it's not what I saw, it's what I felt.

Like rain inside my head. Like a blade. Slicing through flesh. That's how it feels ... around you."

Annoyed, I cry out, "But you barely speak," and my voice seems to float on top of the wind in the forest. The silence around me swallows the sound, and I am soon conscious of the fact that it was only I who spoke out loud. I realize Arik hasn't said a word this entire time—out loud. He stops grinding the bone shovel into the ground and turns his face to my direction, and there, in the haze of his damaged, infected eye, I see a flash, a spark, a thin line of lightning that races there within. We are kin—of the blood of the old ones. There is magic in his blood, and it sings. I rest my head against the oak tree and close my eyes.

I intend to sing back...

I envision a bright light surrounding me, dancing on the edges of my mortal body. It starts up from the ground—the hands of a hundred spirits rising through the depths of the earth and the roots of the trees and the frozen dirt to encompass my physical form. Once it reaches the top of my head, its foggy hands clasp together and engulf me completely—showering me with a silvery mist. The spirit hands forcefully press down on my shoulders locking me in place and slowly creep up my neck, gripping the sides of my face. One of their long, straggly fingers pokes and prods at one of my closed eyelids until they eventually force their way into the socket and wrap around my eyeball. It turns and twists my eyeball like a knob until the fingers pull it out. Only it's not my actual eyeball; it's a projection of my eye—a silver mist duplicate, an astral projection of my physical form. I command the foggy entity to hover over to Arik and engulf him in its glory. In my mind, I send the fingers to his face and implant my mystic eye within his deadened one.

He grunts and groans at the intrusion of my spirit, but I am certain he understands what's happening—that I am gifting him the power of sight, of my sight, albeit temporary.

Paralyzed, I stay at the tree with my back against the trunk. The foggy aura still pulsates around me. I open my working, human eye to see Arik squatting over the open grave with his face in his hands, bewildered, confused. "Open your eye and look at me," I instruct. The excitement is overwhelming. The brands on my arm warm up to the thought of what Arik will see.

"Open your eye," I say again.

Slowly, Arik rises and pulls his hand down from his face, and slowly, the lid of his diseased eye starts to open. He blinks a few times, and his jaw drops when I come into focus. It's like he's seeing for the first time in his life. He tries to speak, but the words get strangled in his throat forcing another grunt and groan.

"Can you see? Can you see me?" I ask.

He nods fervently. I so desperately want to open my other eye so I can experience the astral world as he sees it, but I am not sure of what the repercussions would be. Would it cease the transmission of images? Would I go blind in the process as well? I've never lent my sight to someone before, so the rules are hazy.

"There are no rules. There are never any rules," a growl says to me from beyond the trees.

Startled, my back stiffens at attention. Arik's face twists at the sound as well. "Did you hear that?"

He nods.

"What do you see?" I ask.

Arik opens his mouth again to speak, and again the words don't come out. He is too enraptured with his new gift, too mesmerized by what he can see, that the words refuse to form. But I know they're there, and I need to hear them. I need to know what his eyes see with my sight, so I send another misty hand to hover atop his head, and I use the fingers to dive into his skull. *You*, he thinks, and his voice is so loud I can't tell if it's amplified only in my mind or if it's being projected in the forest. *You're glowing. There is peace and love all around you and inside you. It's so magnificent. You are white and silver. You sit against the tree, but you are the tree. The tree limbs are your veins. They run through you. I see your mother. She sits at your side. Her hand moves up and down your arm. She brands you. Gives you the gift of the words. Ancient words. Words to be spoken for all eternity. There is power in the words, and you can use them to give gifts to others.*

"Like you," I say.

"Like me," he confirms. "I see you, Blodwyn. You are white. Pale like the driven snow with the hair of pure silver. Your body is lean and lithe. You would be a *skjaldmaer*—a fierce and noble warrior—if you were not a heksa." He winces and looks to the ground. "I feel like your power is blinding me again. Like looking at the sun on a bright day. I must look away."

"Surely. But what else do you see? What does the world look like to you through me?"

I pull the spirit hands away from Arik's head, and he gurgles in his throat before speaking aloud, "There is no more darkness. Everything is day now."

I stand up and wave the spirit fog away. In a column of smoke, it retreats into the earth, and I stand up and walk over to him. I place my arms up and touch his shoulders as I cautiously open my closed eye. He lowers his head and rests his forehead on mine as a rush of white light bombards my vision. I am disoriented, off balance. He grabs my waist and steadies my stance. "You see this, don't you?" I ask.

"Aye," he responds.

Flashes of colors pound in my head, fast at first, until they slow themselves to a steady rhythm then fade to a peaceful black. A void. We stare at each other in that void. There is nothingness, darkness. Then like the night sky springing to life, images reappear pulling us out of our collective blindness.

I can see through him.

He can see through me.

"My eyes are your eyes," I say.

"My eyes are your eyes," he replies.

"I don't know how long this will last, but I know how to do it again if we need to."

"Aye," he replies.

We wait a few more hours until we are joined by Aizel, Sorcia, and Ylfa (who carries Trond). We gather around in a circle at the edge of the grave. Aizel places the runestones at the pertinent points of what would have been the star, and Sorcia helps me wrap Modir in white linen. When we're done, Arik lifts the body and places it in the ground. Ylfa's eyes widen when she sees her husband working deftly on his own—amazed that he can navigate perfectly in his perpetual darkness. But he's not in darkness right now. He sees with the brilliance of the light of day through my astral eyes. And he moves as if he's floating—gliding on air, not of this world. A look of worry invades her face for a split second. Worry that her mate has somehow changed and become someone or some*thing* different. And for that split second, I read her. She is loud and clear and dripping with regret and uncertainty—should they have agreed to help me? Was this a big mistake? The baby stirs in the crook of her arm, and she quickly looks away from Arik and down to Trond—her focus now shifted to the task at hand of calming him down.

I stand at the head of the rectangular grave, where Modir's head was gently placed, and I motion for the participants to join hands: Aizel to my right, Sorcia to my left, and Arik directly in front of me at Modir's feet. Ylfa takes a step out from the perimeter and brings the baby over to the tree where they will remain spectators.

"Blodwyn," Aizel whispers, "you're not putting anything in the grave with her? None of her belongings?" She looks to Sorcia with growing concern.

I shake my head. "She doesn't need any of that," I say from the side of my mouth. "I took what I needed from her—locks of her hair, clippings from her nails. Besides, she won't be here very long."

"Yes. You're right," Sorcia interjects. "And we can't make it known that she is here. The punishment alone for defying the council…" Sorcia interjects.

I nod curtly to her, shutting her up, and raise my arms in the air to begin the ritual. "Lo, there do I see my father. Lo, there do I see my mother, and my sisters, and my brothers. Lo, there do I see the line of my people back to the beginning!"

Aizel, Sorcia, and Arik refrain, "Lo, they do call to me. They bid me take my place among them."

A low hum from the forest echoes in my head, and the silver trees frosted with snow sway. They dip their limbs and bow to me, bow in my presence, for they recognize my power. It was I who made the blind man see, and it will be I to make the dead walk again. I cannot commend my mother to the ground with the words of our people. This is just a temporary state for her, and I'm afraid that if I close out the traditional prayer, it will seal her to the other realm, and she will not be able to pass through when I call for her again. I'm supposed to finish the ritual with *In the halls of Valhalla, where the brave may live forever*, but I can't. I tightly close my eyes and listen to the music coming from beyond the trees, from beyond the sky. A low beating drum that plays in rhythmic time just for me—for my pleasure, for my knowledge. And that music makes me sway like the supplicating trees. It fills me with delight as the words come to me. "In the wild of the forest, here she will rest until it is time for her to rise again and seek forever."

Sorcia makes a gasping noise in her throat. Aizel's body stiffens. The runes on my right arm get hot, and my left arm feels heavy, weighted down. It takes all my strength to hold it above my head. "And she will come when I call for her. She will retake her place as the Blodheksa and usher in the new age of time." The pressure in my arm is too much to bear, and I drop both down to my sides and end the ceremony. The other participants release their grasp, and Arik starts filling the grave back with dirt.

"Blodwyn? What was that?" Aizel asks, her voice wrought with concern and fear.

"Come, sisters," I say and outstretch my arms to gobble them both up in an embrace. I bring each one close to my cheeks and press their faces hard against my own, so as to be one with them in body and mind. And I speak to them without my voice, penetrating their conscious souls with the words of our ancestors. *You both are my strength. All things we can do together. I could never repay you for the support you have given me during this time, and I love you both dearly. And I know you mourn as well. But fear not, Modir is not gone. She is with us three and with Trond. With her body in the ground, her power will go into the earth. Into every leaf. Every tree. Every scoop of soil from here to miles beyond. Her power will spread far and wide. And when the day comes, I promise I will call her back to rule. I know what I must do, yet I know not how to do it. In good time, it will be revealed to us. She speaks to me still, and I know she will continue to guide me. To guide us.*

And with that I take a step back and roll up the sleeve of my left arm revealing more fresh tattoos—the runes of the ancients, the words of my mother—branded in black from my wrist to shoulder.

Aizel's eyes grow wide and round in amazement. "I'm going to have to take a closer look at that, Blodwyn. I think we should get back to the cave."

Chapter Five

In the Time of Darkness
In the Age of Ice
Wintertime, 666 AD
The Crystal Cave, North of the Frostheim Forest
Afternoon of the New Moon

When we had gotten back to the cave the night of Modir's burial, Aizel spent hours inspecting my new brands. Back and forth, she twisted my arms from side to side. Up and down. She examined and read aloud every inch of flesh that was tattooed with runes. Sorcia gasped and "ahhh-ed" as she too tried to commit the words to memory. I didn't need to, as they were not only on me, but also they were *in* me. I heard the story in my head like whispers in the night. Aizel had marveled at the markings, noting that the story had changed a little on my right arm.

"What do you mean, changed?" I had inquired.

"I can't say exactly. It's almost as if there are more details in some weird way. Look here!" She held up my right hand in the firelight of the cave.

"Your fingers now have marks. They weren't there before."

She was right. The entirety of my hands were now covered in runes. I hadn't noticed that.

"Regardless," she continued, "this is incredible. I need to study this further and copy what is written on you. Every change, every new appearance. These are your mother's words, Blodwyn. These are the ancient's words! The old ones speak through you, now. It is a sign."

She pored over me for another hour or so, scribbling fiercely on the surface of our wooden altar. Finally, I desired rest and told her I could endure no more—that she would have to continue a different night. She was cross at first but understood and eventually relented.

In the days that followed, Arik stayed close to my side. He and I were virtually inseparable as we adjusted to the scope and sequence of our new vision abilities. We quickly learned that the farther apart we were, the less intense the vision became for both of us, yet even so, we were able to view the world through each other. When he saw the world with his new sight, I was able to see, like double vision, in my mind's eye. The images from him, and my own ability to see was like a side-by-side picture of separate events unfolding at once. At first, discerning the multiple vantage points was confusing and jarring. It made me dizzy, and in the beginning, left me with a pounding headache. Arik saw things in bright, white light, and it was initially overwhelming. As the days went on, I gradually adjusted to the point where if we weren't together, I felt empty and lost.

It was a matter of a day or two until Arik was sleeping next to me in my chamber of the cave. With the understanding that Ylfa needed to tend to Trond, that Arik and I were experimenting with his new astral sight, she hesitantly allowed it. In all honesty, there was nothing for her to be worried or jealous over, for I had no feelings of desire for her husband. Arik made me feel warm and safe. As the son of a *seidr*, a practitioner of some of the most ancient magics, his primal blood sang songs to my own, and I regarded him as a kindred spirit. His soul spoke to mine, and in our combined vision, in our shared new world, we became one—that which was beyond the joining of a man and wife.

At night, I would lay my head against his bare chest and run my fingers across each of his thick pink and purple battle scars—outlining them, tracing them, deciphering the code that made Arik *Arik*. He would smooth my hair away from my face, soft and gentle touches, until we both fell asleep in each other's arms. And as soon as our consciousnesses drifted to that other realm of sleep, the images would begin. Our nighttime dreams danced and mingled together producing glorious stories on a shared level. Woven tapestries of light and beauty unfolded in our minds— filling us with haunting images and macabre lullabies of the old gods. We saw the perfect world we had longed to create, and it was pure, intoxicating magic—so intoxicating that I often wished to sleep forever.

But endless sleep with endless dreams was not to be. And thus, during the waking hours, we used our shared sight to our advantage in many ways. When Arik hunted, having me in the general area as a lookout gave him better insight into his prey, and during spellwork and rituals, *he* served as *my* lookout and guard. My shield. My protector. Soon, Arik and I went nowhere without each other.

Arik had tracked a herd of deer to the northernmost region of our cave, and we have been traversing across the frozen landscape for the last three days. Even though the deer in this herd are small, just one of them will provide enough tasty meat to feed the five of us for at least four days. Plus, I will get much use from the heart of the beast, the blood, the pelt—just one of these animals will be beneficial to our clan, and Arik plans on bringing more than just one home with us.

This area in the north is serene. It feels as if we are away from the entire world. The air is crisp and the ground is unpolluted by the machinations of man. Everything is white—frost and ice for miles in every direction—the only indication of life are the hoof tracks of the herd, and our foot tracks close behind them. This place is utterly undisturbed. Not even the nomadic tribes venture this far north. I am glad for it, for if they had, they might want to spike down their tents and rape this pristine land as they did to every other place they traveled.

There is something sacred in being here. Peaceful. Enthralling. Modir had brought me here a few times when I was a child, and I remembered the layout of the land well. She had taken me to a cavern she called The Crystal Cave. It was a small opening in the hillside hidden by an icy waterfall. We had taken an obscure path around the hill that led to the opening behind the deluge. Inside, I understood why it was called The Crystal Cave—for everything shone with white glittery frost crystals. In the center of the cave, there was a pool of fresh water, steaming with the natural heat of the deep earth. Modir had brought me there to teach me about frostwork—how to manipulate ice and water. I wasn't the best student in that area, so my lessons were limited. Frostwork was more Sorcia's expertise. Besides, Mother always said I was better with fire.

Much better…

I think about that cave and realize it would be a good place for us to rest after the hunt. "If we…" I start to say, but Arik whips his head around and places his finger on his lips to silence me. The echo of my two words rings in the frigid air, and a flock of birds flies off from a snowy treetop. Arik eyes me contentiously, I mouth "Sorry," and we push forward. Tracking. Stalking. Hunting.

I slow down some and take in the white world around me. I am mesmerized by how my thick, smoky breath indicates a frigid sting in the temperature, yet my inner core feels as if it's ablaze. I feel as if I could walk naked in this forest and not be affected by the cold. I kneel in the dusty snow and wave my arms above the ground in a circle around me. Instantly, the snow melts as if I am a human torch, and I glance behind me to see a melted path left in my wake like a little stream at my feet.

When I look back up and ahead of me, Arik is a far distance away. His body sways back and forth like a dot across the horizon, and suddenly, his form is swallowed into the open arms of the forest trees. I call out "Arik!" and surprise even myself at the timbre of fear that comes from my lips as a split second of hysteria catches in my throat.

It's just the cold, I think.

Arik doesn't respond or turn around, so I call out to him again, and still, his form doesn't manifest back into my line of sight. I close my eyes to try to see through him, to try to penetrate his mind's eye with my urgent cry, but he is closed off from me. I cannot see through him. Our shared space is dark, and now the panic grows heavy in my chest, and the brands on my arms pulse hot with my rapid heartbeat—the *thum thum, thum thum* quickens with every second that passes.

Thum thum, thum thum in my chest—like my heart is about to explode.

Thum thum, thum thum racing up and down both my arms—like something underneath the skin ready to tear away from my body.

Why are his eyes closed? Why can't he see me?
I think frantically and take off running towards the tree line. The thick layer of snow beneath my feet slows me down as flashes of Arik's vision start to come into view and strike my brain like flashes of lightning. His white light pierces me—fast and painful, like a serpent striking its prey. Yet I run, frenzied and desperate, praying he isn't in danger, praying my distance from him hasn't caused him to go blind again and put him in peril.

The deer.

Arik's arm raised.

The beast's eyes wide.

Blade reflects the winter sun.

I see it. He sees it. And I realize he purposefully shut me out so as to not be distracted by me.

Because he can do this without my help.

I hear the deer's bleating wail as the blade descends on it—both ringing in my head and carried on the crisp air. Another flash from Arik's vision mixed with the sound of the animal's death cry disorients me so much that I stumble over some bramble and fall face first into the snow—into the slush pile around me. I bite my lower lip to prevent myself from crying out so as to not disturb Arik's hunt, but the pain from my twisted ankle makes me see stars. If it's not broken, it's badly sprained at the least. I close my eyes and suck down the pain. I don't want to distract him with my accident because *I* know, if *he* knows I'm in distress, he will abandon the mutilation and the promise of food and rush to my side.

Chapter Five

So, here I sit—in the cold (but not in the cold), waiting for my companion to rescue me.

I try to stand up, but my attempt is futile. The bone in my ankle is like crushed granite in a linen sack—ground up fragments rubbing against each other. The searing pain, like hot pokers in my calf, forces me to sit back down against a tree. I wince. *This is going to be harder than I thought.* I quickly realize it is going to take much more than my sheer will alone to heal this. An injury of this magnitude will need some assistance, so I relax myself and wait it out for Arik. I'm not sure what role he can play in mending my leg, and although I've borne witness to his brute strength, I'm not sure he will be able to carry both the deer and me three days back to our cave. *But maybe if I can get to The Crystal Cave...* The thought makes me wince again. I bite my lower lip to stifle the agony down and inhale through my nose. My chest puffs up, breasts heave underneath my heavy cloak, and I savor the slow, calming exhale out of my mouth.

And when I think I can't stand the pain a moment longer, I look up to see Arik before me. *I am saved!* The sun shines brightly behind him, filtering through his loose strands of orange hair. It illuminates the space around his figure like a golden halo, like a mystic wood god manifesting from the depths of the snowy forest.

He extends his hand to me, and I shake my head furiously. "I can't," I squeak with defeat, a part of me rife with embarrassment.

He extends both hands to me. "No, Arik. I think it's broken," I say angrily.

He grunts and huffs. Puffs of billowy white smoke emit from both his nose and mouth as he bends forward, scoops me at my waist, and hoists me over his broad shoulder.

We need to go to The Crystal Cave behind the waterfall, I say directly into his mind.

My head flashes with the white light of his acknowledgment, and he sturdies my body one last time before pressing forward. My white hair hangs down the length of his bulky back, and I see the deer. He has tied its front legs together and wrapped the opposite end of the long rope around his waist. The beast drags in the snow behind us, and I stare at its cold black eyes for the duration of our sojourn to the cave.

The inside of the cavern glistens. A sheet of ice coats the gray and black rock, and from the mouth behind the waterfall, the sunlight refracts the light of the glittery frost and speckles of water creating a shadowy, strobing effect throughout. It's just as I remembered from the last time I was here with Modir. There's about forty feet of stone floor before reaching the edge of the cave pool. Arik unties the rope from his waist and drops the carcass near the opening. Then he carries me to the pond and gently lowers me down at the water's edge. The warmth of the water steams up in thin misty columns, and I quickly undress, eager to submerge my body in it, eager to bring my ankle some relief. My fingers stumble with every frantic unbuttoning and unfastening—I can't get my clothes off fast enough! The skin on my ankle has already become swollen and tight, and it throbs with a deep and painful pink hue. Arik turns his head away from my nakedness in a respectful gesture to my privacy, but he doesn't close his eyes. I know the astral light between us allows him to see all of me, but to be honest, I don't mind.

The second the water touches my leg, I sigh. The pressure from the injury seems to melt away in the weightlessness of the pool. I relax my muscles and lower my entire body within.

Arik kneels beside the rock bank when I am fully concealed in the water. "Better?" he asks.

"So much better," I sigh.

"Good."

He puts his hand in the water and swirls it around. I raise my eyebrows in curiosity. "Thinking of hopping in?" I ask coyly.

His hand goes rigid, and he quickly removes it from the water with a grunt.

"It's fine. I wouldn't mind," I say, dipping my chin down and putting a little bit of water in my mouth. "You hauled me and a dead animal through the snow. You've been working for these last three days in the most treacherous conditions. I wouldn't fault you for wanting to join me. You should. It's very relaxing. And besides, you could use a little downtime before we head back."

His face twists with hesitation, but by the slight smirk at the corner of his mouth, it's plain to see the thought had entered his mind.

"Come on!" I press him. "How different is it from sleeping next to each other every night?"

He grimaces once more as the idea wrestles in his mind one last time. Then finally, he gets up and disrobes. When he is fully undressed and has made a pile of both of our clothes, he stands at the edge of the pool and looks at me with a glance of final hesitation. I take in the sight of him—his bulky stature, his legs that resembled tree trunks. I was all too familiar with the look and feel of his bare chest, but the rest of his flesh had been a mystery to me until now. He was the villagers' version of their god Thor—a *rekkr*, a warrior, with a strong, sturdy body. I found myself shocked at the massive organ between his legs—the girth and heft of it (even in its sleeping state) had to be irritating for him to heave around daily. The crevice between my own legs tickles, so I quickly push those thoughts from my mind. I move over in the water giving him plenty of space to submerge in.

He cranes his neck back and lets out a long, pleasurable sigh. I smile at him. "See! When I'm right, I'm right."

He smiles back as he dips his shoulders down low. "You were right," he relents.

I laugh and splash water in his direction. He wipes his face with the back of his hand and chuckles back. I've never heard that noise from him before, and its deep sound booms in the cave.

Suddenly, there's movement from underneath the rocks at the bank of the pool, and I back away from the edge, startled. "What was that?" I ask, worried.

Arik's face twists with concern, and he puts a hand up as if to silence me. He cocks his head, and we hear it again—a shuffling sound that surrounds the circumference of the pool. He reaches over, grabs me at the waist and pulls me up against him. "Vipers," he whispers into my ear. His breath is warm against my skin, and it sends a shiver throughout my body. "They stay by the rocks under the pool for the heat."

Mesmerized, I wiggle from his grasp and swim to the side. "Vipers," I say. "I've never seen one."

"Blodwyn, wait!" he protests, but it's already too late. There on the edge of the pool, curled up and waiting to greet me, are two serpents— one white and one black. Their tongues flick out wildly at me as they sense my presence. The white one with the iridescent pink eyes dips its head cautiously in my direction. I prop my arms up on the rocks, extend the lower half of my body out, and gaze dreamily at the snakes before me.

"Blodwyn, be careful. They're deadly," Arik says as he swims up next to me. He puts his arm underneath mine, readying himself to pull me back into the water to safety if the animals get too close.

They won't hurt you, a voice gurgles in my head, and Arik squeezes my shoulder. He heard it, too.

"They won't hurt me," I repeat, and he relaxes his grip.

Be not afraid, it says. *I go before you, always.*

The white viper turns its head to the black viper and slithers forward an inch. The black viper languidly moves off the rock shelf and retreats to the darkness. The white one turns its attention back to me. It raises its head and dances back and forth, a slow to-and-fro movement that hypnotizes me. Entrances me. Excites me. I am overwhelmed with desire. A need. I want to feel the snake all over my body—across my skin, wrapping around my breasts. Suddenly, as if from nowhere, images of Arik's naked body flood my mind. And I feel a hunger grow. A hunger for him. To know him. To feel him. To have him...

I scarcely realize my legs gyrate in time with the animal's motions. *What are you doing?* Arik asks, but it's not out loud. He speaks directly to my mind.

The water is warm and inviting and the snake moves with such grace and ease. It speaks to me with its pink eyes and with its white skin and with its every move. The crevice between my legs throbs. As I sway in the water, the folds of my skin there tickle as the little current hits them. Arik watches me intently. He stares at the arch of my back, the sway of my hips, the bouncing of my backside as I lift it up and down in the water.

I look over to him, and his face flushes pink— pink with desire and curiosity and shame. His manhood strengthens. The tip of it jabs my hip bone, and he quickly pulls away from me. I spread my legs in the water and look behind me, then back at him. His face flushes again.

"I've known men before," I say and wiggle around. "I've known men before and never bore. That's how I know I'm not the Blodheksa." I say out loud as if to make this alright.

He pauses, drinks the vision of me in, and in my head, I see how *he* sees *me*—white, golden, snow, water, peace, love, safety. More than flesh. More than a body. He sees me as *entity*, as all-encompassing. He runs his fingers down the length of my spine, stops at the top of my backside, then moves down the side of my hip to the side of my thigh. I wiggle again. With his other hand, he cups one of my breasts underwater and rolls my pink nipple in between two fingers. I moan instinctually but never break the gaze of my serpent.

"I need you to," I say to Arik... I say to the snake. Arik lets go of my chest and moves behind me in the pool. He spreads my legs and inches closer in between—closer to my opening, closer to the jewel of my womanhood. The tip of his organ grazes my inner thigh, and I can't help but writhe against it. The snake moves. I move. Arik grabs onto my hips for leverage and gently slides himself into me.

And we dance.

In perfect rhythm in the water, we dance. I prop my arms up on the rocks as Arik pumps himself slowly, easily in me. His movements aren't the normal in-and-out thrusts I'd experienced before.

Not the pounding, jerky motions of lesser men I have known. The entirety of Arik's organ, accompanied by a rush of water, fills me completely. His movements are like quick jabs on my inside. Every ridge of his organ touches hidden spots in me like keys opening locks for the first time. He rides me like a sea god, like a mighty being penetrating his subject, hard and deep, yet smooth and gentle. We are wet and slick, and sliding, and one. His hands touch me everywhere they can reach. He kneads my backside, a thumb dangerously close to the opening, but never going in.

A blinding light from our shared vision rocks us both, sends me into a fit of ecstasy, and my legs tighten and my sex clamps down on him when I reach the culmination of my pleasure. Quickly, he releases himself from inside me. I turn my head back to ask why, to ask if he'd finished. Arik holds his organ tight at the base, pumps his hand up and down on it a few times, and spills himself into the pool.

I flip myself around. "Why did you..." I start to ask but suddenly stop myself. Maybe it's the heat of the spring, or the aftermath of my pleasure, or the long journey we've endured, or the hypnotism of the serpent, but what I see, what I witness, causes me to blink rapidly in disbelief.

And nothing surprises me.

But there, in the water, between Arik's legs, he holds a white serpent in his hand. A white serpent instead of his organ. A white serpent instead of his manhood. It flicks out its forked tongue then coils back to its original human, manhood shape. My eyes go wide, and he swims up next to me and holds my back steady in the prone position with one hand. With his other hand, he touches my stomach and circles the silver tuft of hair at my crevice.

The white serpent from the rock is now on me... on my neck. It slithers down my chest and curls atop my breast, which floats above the water. My body tenses in fear of this deadly animal on me, but I am distracted when Arik slides his finger inside, playing with me in a teasing way. *It won't hurt you*, the faraway voice gurgles again.

"It won't hurt you," Arik repeats. "This is how we'll truly know if you're the Blodheksa."

He lifts me higher up from my back so that the front of my body is completely out of the water. A blast of cold air rolls through the cave, and I shiver from the sudden chill. Arik uses his fore and middle fingers to separate the flesh of my sex apart. The snake slithers down my chest, to my abdomen, then turns its head around and makes its way back up to meet my gaze. Its tongue flicks my nipple with feathery-like kisses, and it raises its head to stare at me with its pearly pink eyes. The entire length of its body spans down my body, its thick tail rubbing against the outer ridges of my sex. The cool snakeskin engulfs me, presses on me with its lower weight, and I can't help but be excited. Like I can come to pleasure yet again if given just... one... more... minute.

The snake slithers its tail further down me, and Arik spreads my legs wider, and my nether lips further apart. Without warning, the viper wriggles its tail inside me. Unlike the grooves and ridges of a man's organ, the serpent is slick and smooth, and it curls itself in me and on me with a powerful pressure grip. Arik lets go of my folds and uses both his hands to support my body. He bends forward, kisses one of my breasts, and bites the nipple.

And the serpent moves in and out of me. Its body not only jabs my opening like a man would, but it also presses itself down on my outer pearl for a double sensation of ecstasy.

Extreme ecstasy.

Inhuman ecstasy.

Godly ecstasy.

The serpent penetrates me in such a way that it's hard to breathe. Like it's strangling me from the inside. I am light-headed. Mystified. My body goes limp and numb with pleasure as I reach the pinnacle of delight over, and over, and over again until the pleasure starts to morph into pain.

I keep my eyes closed, but Arik sends me what he sees. There are vipers everywhere—lined up all around the edge of the cave pool. Brown ones, black ones, striped ones, speckled ones. Hundreds of them. Darting their tongues. Hissing. Gyrating. Poised and ready. Each one waits for a chance to penetrate me. Each one wants a chance to feel me from the inside. Each one wants to please me more than the other, to be the head chieftain of my *thviet*. Each one wants to fuck me.

I call out with one final wail of delight, and Arik lowers my body back into the water. The white serpent slithers up my chest and out of my sex. It hisses at the others, and they all scurry away. Arik positions himself behind me. My back relaxes against his chest, and we both sigh.

And suddenly I realize, my ankle no longer hurts.

Chapter Six

In the Time of Darkness
In the Age of Ice
Wintertime, 666 AD
Caverns in the Far North
Late Afternoon of the Waxing Crescent Moon

The light of the setting sun sprinkles in through the mouth of our cave, and as Arik and I step into the vestibule, our bodies make the rays of light flicker throughout the center area. Aizel and Sorcia sit by the low burning fire in almost a huddle. Their voices mumble secrets that sound like running water in the river or a downpour of rain on a summer afternoon.

"Hello?" I announce as I draw closer.

The two perk up from their hunched position, scramble to their feet, race over to me, and nearly take me down with a tight bear hug. I wiggle away a little, then lean my head in so that we all touch foreheads. I flash sparkling waves of white light into them, and they both smile. I smile back, but then they are both on me again in a fierce embrace.

Chapter Six

"Blodwyn! To the gods! We were so worried about you!" Sorcia says frantically, her face buried in my neck.

I bring both my hands up to rub their backs simultaneously. "It's fine. It's fine. I'm fine." My left hand stops at Sorcia's shorn locks. I grip what little of it is left within my palm and tug at it. She pulls her face up from the crook of my neck and eyes me coolly. I briefly narrow my eyes back at her with a look that lets her know I haven't forgotten—I haven't forgotten her botched love spell in the woods, and I will deal with it very soon.

"Three moon phases, Blodwyn!" Aizel bellows, breaking my and Sorcia's stare.

"I'm back. I'm here now."

Sorcia places a hand on her hip and bounces on the weight of her leg. "But where were you? Why were you gone so long?"

I swivel my head to Arik behind me. He releases all the game we've hunted onto the floor with a deafening *thud*. Then he unties the deer from his waistband, and its legs crash loudly to the ground. Aizel and Sorcia both shudder instinctively from the sound. "We'll be good for the rest of the winter," I say, trying to reassure them. "We went up to the Crystal Cave. I knew the land would be plentiful, and we have mouths to feed." I look back again at Arik and nod. "Many mouths."

"The Crystal Cave?" Sorcia repeats with a tone of disbelief.

I ignore her.

Aizel grabs my upper arm. "Blodwyn, is everything alright? We tried to contact you. On the astral light. But you were dark, and…"

"It's Arik. When I'm connected through him, there really isn't much else I see or tune in to. We're still adjusting, and…"

"We need to talk," Sorcia interjects.

Aizel looks at her sharply, then back at me. Both their faces darken with concern. "Can it wait? I need to see Trond. Where's baby Ruz?" I say excitedly.

Again, with the ominous glances—so ominous that it makes my stomach tumble.

"What's going on?" I demand.

Aizel grips both of my shoulders. "We need to talk about Trond, too."

Panic hits the back of my throat. "What do you mean? Where is he? Is he well?"

"He's fine. He's in the alcove with Ylfa, but…" Aizel pauses, takes a breath, and eyes Arik over my shoulder. Looking deeply into my eyes, she tries to needle her way into my mind like a thousand little pinpricks desperately trying to penetrate my brain.

I frantically shake my head back and forth to break her astral hold. "No!" I say, forcefully. "Whatever you have to say, you can say in front of him!"

Aizel drops her head down and speaks softly. "It's Ylfa. She's… she's…" she stutters.

"Changed," Sorcia blurts.

Chapter Six

I can feel Arik stiffen behind me as if his senses went on extreme alert. "What do you mean, *changed*?"

"I'm not certain, but it's something I thought could possibly happen," Aizel shifts her weight from leg to leg. "You see, Blodwyn, Trond is the child of the Blodheksa. He has great power. Every time he feeds, he draws a little more of Ylfa into himself—her energy, her spirit. Her heart and soul are... are..." She struggles for the right word.

"Darkening," Sorcia finishes.

Arik moves forward with great concern and stands next to me.

I shake my head again. "Wait. Is Ylfa dying? Are you saying Trond is killing her?"

Aizel shuffles again. "No. Not killing."

"Changing," Sorcia repeats.

"Changing, how?" Arik pipes in.

"She's different, Blodwyn," Aizel emphasizes. "Withdrawn. Reclusive."

"She doesn't want to talk to us or interact with us. She just wants to nurse the babe," Sorcia adds. "And she's very vocal about not letting us near him. Angry."

"Violent," Aizel whispers.

"And you say you knew this would happen? How?" I pressure.

Aizel's gaze drifts to the corner of the room where the main altar is—as if she's remembering something, *hearing* something, like something is pushing through space and time and speaking only to her, through her. She closes her eyes and inhales that vivid memory. When she exhales through her mouth, her breath smells sweet, like fruit, like berries on the vine. A quick smirk invades the side of her mouth then quickly dissolves back into her tight-lipped frown of worry. This makes me furious with curiosity: *What did she see? What did she hear? What was she privy to that I wasn't?* "I didn't know for sure, but it was always in my mind as a possibility. Your mother had spoken of something like this happening. But Ylfa is strong…"

"Robust," Sorcia interjects.

Aizel rolls her eyes. "And with a child of her own so close in age—a child whose father is the son of a seidr…"

All eyes briefly transfix on Arik, and his back stiffens from all the attention. He hates it.

"Is this affecting Trond?" I ask.

"No. I don't think so. The child is thriving. Trond has gotten fat in such a short time!"

"Yet, Ylfa has lost much weight in such a short time," Sorcia chimes.

I look at her and narrow my eyes again in disdain.

Aizel's gaze shifts to the ground. "Since you left."

I break from Aizel's grasp, and I force my way passed her. "I'm going to see them," I huff, and Arik falls in step right behind me.

"Wait, Blodwyn!" Aizel calls.

I turn my head back to look at her.

"There's something else."

"It's going to have to wait, Aizel. I need to see my brother."

Arik grabs my elbow and moves with me through the corridor of the cave. He stops just before we reach the opening and looks at me with a loving expression. His cloudy eye and other-worldly sight bounce images of *me* back to my mind. His vision of me ... and him. Him and me dancing naked under the snow-capped trees on a night of the full moon. Him and me embracing in the pool in the Crystal Cave. Him and me wrapping our bodies together like snakes in the grass with the night sky bursting open with a thousand stars. It disorients me for a second—makes me feel unsteady on my feet, and I close my eyes and shake my head, ceasing the transmission of his daydream. "But she's your wife!" I scold in a hushed tone.

"Is she though?" he whispers. "She's not anymore. Not really."

"Have you no feeling left for her? No consideration?"

"Blodwyn, we..."

I wave my hand in the air, dismissing him. "We were hypnotized. The serpents speak with a strange tongue. We should have never..."

Quickly he puts a hand over my mouth, the thick padding of his palm clamps my lips together. "Don't," he commands.

Angrily, I bite him. "Don't!" I scold when he retreats from the sting.

"I was sent to you. I am committed to you. I am in debt to you. It is through you that this world will be cleansed, and I am to be the one to guide you to what needs to be done. I am your instrument, your conduit, your second set of eyes. Do not make light of the power that stems from us, for to do so would be to deny thyself." He speaks psychically to me in the tongue of the ancients. I absorb his words and nod.

We enter the alcove together. Ylfa sits in the wooden chair gazing at Trond in her lap. He is wrapped tightly in his blanket and rests in the crook of her arm. She's humming a soft tune and drops kisses on top of his head. Her motherly instincts are on high alert because she pipes up when she senses our presence in the room. "Oh!" she gasps. "You startled me!" She jumps up and scurries over to us in the threshold. "Husband!" she gushes. "You've been gone but so long!"

"Wife," he addresses her and kisses her forehead.

She seems to recoil when his lips touch her face. With babe in hand, she backs up a few inches and scowls at us. "Too long," she practically growls, and it's so un-Ylfa-like that it sends a cold chill down my back. Aizel and Sorcia were right. She is changed. She is much thinner than when we left, and her skin is an ashen color—haggard and fatigued.

I move closer to her, feign a smile, and raise my voice an octave so I sound more pleasant to her ears. "Oh yes! The hunt was quite arduous, but we were blessed with good game and an array of herbs and spices. We'll have plenty to go around for all of us for the rest of the winter."

The sides of her mouth extend upward in a wide smile—an unnatural smile. An overly exaggerated grin that is almost frightening to look at. "Of course. And how wonderful that is to hear! I am thankful for you, Blodwyn Solvven—thankful for your friendship and for everything you've done for my Arik. Without his sight, he would not have been able to hunt. Without the hunt, we would not have sustenance. So, thank you. Thank you for the glorious gift you've bestowed upon all of us."

I smile back, harder, trying to mask my uneasiness. "Make no mention of it. It was the least that I could do. The gift you've given *me* is priceless. If not for you, I don't know what would have become of my sweet Ruz."

At the mention of my brother's name, Ylfa nervously looks down to him and takes a step back.

"You saved his life, Ylfa. That is a debt that cannot be repaid in full."

Another step back. A pained expression washes over her—darkens her visage, makes her eyes look weary yet wild. "It's my pleasure," she mumbles, and again, she steps back, pulling away and creating an uncomfortable distance between her and me.

Between Trond and me.

Now *my* instincts kick in, and I'm more than uneasy—more than uncomfortable with the situation unfolding before me. I extend my arms out to her, and the edges of my sleeves creep up past my wrists revealing my rune imprints. "I'll take him now," I say, trying to keep my voice steady, but the tattoos on my arms start to throb.

She looks at him, then back up at me. Panic sets into her chest, and she lets out a short, stunted sigh and nervously bounces the children in her arms. "Oh, no need. He's fine where he is. Little man will be eating soon anyway."

"Now, now," I say, remaining calm. "I've been away long enough. I need some time with my brother, as you need some time with Arik. Besides, I think that plump babe can take a little break from a timed feeding." I step closer to her.

Ylfa lets out a nervous laugh and speaks with a rushed, heightened voice. "Don't be ridiculous! What you need is to rest from your travels, sister. It'll do you some..."

"I insist," I growl, but my voice fills the entire chamber with a hollow sound. The runes burn against my flesh, and through Arik's vantage point, I see my eyes glowing red.

Ylfa gasps again, hesitates, then reluctantly places Trond in my arm. He smells of berries — sweet and succulent. Like the same smell from Aizel's breath moments before.

Modir...

I snuggle him close to my face and shower him with hundreds of kisses. He coos and squirms with delight at my touch. "I'm home, Ruz. Søster is home." I turn on my heel and shift the baby tighter in my grasp. "We'll be back to feed later,"

Chapter Six

I call over my shoulder and walk out. And again, Arik is right at my side, walking out with me. Ylfa opens her mouth to say something in protest, but we're halfway down the corridor before the words come out.

"Told you," Arik grumbles, and I snuggle the baby closer to my chest with a near-death grip. Angry, thankful, relieved—a tumult of emotion swirls inside my body. I am disturbed by both Ylfa's appearance and behavior. Disturbed and saddened to think: is this my fault? The string of unfortunate events unravels before me—Ylfa would not have changed if not for Trond, and if not for Trond, Modir would still be here, and...

I grip Trond tighter as if to pulverize the thought from my head. Trond is not the reason for Modir's death. I know that. It's not his fault it took him seventeen years to be born or that her body just couldn't sustain the trauma of labor with him. It's no one's fault. There's no blame to be doled out. And I think that's where a good portion of my anger stems from—the fact that there is no guilty party in the matter, no one to exact revenge upon, no one to pay for my loss.

Because if there was, it would lessen this pain.

As I walk through the cave, I can still feel her presence all around me. Her voice, her voluminous laugh, still echo in the chambers. Her laugh was distinct, infectious. The buoyancy in its sound was like rolling waves crashing on the shore. Once she started laughing, everyone around her did too. They didn't even have to know why she was laughing, or what was so funny—the mere sound of her joy was enough to delight others. And she was wise. She knew things in her soul—things that she had never even been taught. There was an innate knowledge of the world and her surroundings and her body and the bodies of others. The blood of the ancients spoke loudly to her and gifted her with inherent talents. Modir tried hard to instill those lessons in me, and Aizel, and Sorcia, and all the other downtrodden children she claimed as her own, for she had wanted to raise the next generation to survive the cleansing and prosper in her new world.

But she's not gone, I think. *Not really*.

And suddenly, her passing doesn't feel real to me. It feels like a dream. Like it never really happened, and I'm on the edge of waking up and all will be right in the world again. She's in the front chamber with Aizel talking about the herbs they picked. Or she's at the altar with Sorcia laughing about how idiotic the woodworker's hair looked yesterday when they went into the village.

But when we reach the chamber, the absence of her voice, of her laugh, strikes me deep in the chest, and the runes on my arms flash with a searing heat.

"No child should be without their mother," I snarl.

"You'll fill in for a while," Arik responds, matter-of-factly. His voice is confident—sure that I will be a proper substitute.

I glance at him from the corner of my eye and sigh. I suppose I will have to be a temporary replacement until I can raise her up from the ground. Because I can. And I will. I will move the heavens and the earth and rip the cosmos apart, so help me! And when I do, she will rain fire down upon this place—scorch the earth and all in its wake. Cleanse the land so the old ones can roam free again, and the three of us—Modir, Trond, me—we will serve our gods faithfully in the paradise we have created. In pleasure and pain for all eternity. And if that doesn't happen, I don't care! As long as she is back with me, I would live the rest of my days in this living hell of ice and snow if it meant we could be together again.

"Until she comes back again," Arik interrupts my thoughts, but he says it in a knowing tone as if he had been reading my mind and sensing my mounting rage.

I ignore him and continue to the vestibule where Aizel and Sorcia are waiting.

When we enter the chamber, they immediately rush over with *ooohs* and *aaahhs* as if it's been days since they have seen the boy. *Because it has been.*

"Oh, Blodwyn!" Sorcia gushes with excitement. "Let me hold him!"

Aizel punches her shoulder. "Sister! Let her have a moment!" she scolds.

I walk by both and sit on the floor by the fire. Trond wiggles in time with my movements before settling in comfortably against me. The three join me by the fire, and the tone once again grows dire.

"You needed to talk?" I ask, fixated on the babe, but I can feel Sorcia's black eyes staring at me from across the blaze.

"Sorcia's love spell failed," Aizel blurts.

"Like I knew it would," I answer.

Sorcia exhales. "But it created a problem."

"Like I said it would," I reiterate. "You know how much I hate doing love spells. And then, you went off on your own and said some unsanctioned words…"

"Unsanctioned?" she cries.

I look up from Trond and glare at her. "Yes, Sorcia. You heard me. Unsanctioned. As in, words and actions that have never been performed in those types of spells before."

"I don't need your permission to do spellwork, Blodwyn!" she exclaims. "I've seen *you* do plenty of *un*sanctioned things. Need I remind you of your mother's funeral!"

"Sorcia!" Aizel yells, silencing her. "Swallow your words!" She takes a breath and collects herself. "Blodwyn, because the spell failed, Grom has expressed he no longer wants the company of Sorcia."

I eye Sorcia harshly. "At what point would you like for me to say I told you so?"

Stupid love spell. Should have listened to my gut.

She returns my glare. Her anger and pain shoot out at me like sharp blades stabbing my chest and back. But I ignore her vicious glances. "And…" I say, my voice giving way for Aizel to continue.

"Not an *and*. More like a *because*. Because of the timing of the spell and the birth of Trond and the loss of Modir and asking Grom to help… well…" she trails, "it's created a serious situation. Grom has vowed to tell the Jarl of Frostheim what we asked him to do."

"If he hasn't done so already," Sorcia chimes.

My back stiffens, and Arik catches on to my posture shift.

"The Jarl went on a raid with his group around the same time the two of you left for the hunt," Aizel says.

"Why would the Jarl go on a raid? That doesn't make sense," I say. "He's the chieftain, the most important figurehead in the village. Why would he risk his life for some trivial invasion?"

"Apparently, his wife said he was bored and wanted some excitement. Like from his old days," Sorcia adds.

Aizel sighs. "Anyway, if Grom hasn't already gotten his ear, he will soon."

I look to Arik sharply. Desperately. He nods at me with acknowledgement of my panic. Already, the wheels begin to turn through our collective mind. Each possible solution to this possible devastating problem ticks off one by one between us— *burn the village? No. Move the family? No. Move the body? No…*

"The implications for all of us…"

My head feels like it's underwater, and the room feels as if it's spinning. I am dizzy and drowning as the possibilities crash over and into me like a hard-packed avalanche. For a second I want to cry out—I want my mother! She would know what to do. And now she's gone, abandoned the boy and me in our time of need. And I can't control the wave of despair that infiltrates my heart. I am so angry and sad, there isn't a word to explain this… this… void inside of me. This desperate, uncontrollable ache that pushes up against my chest almost splitting me in two separate sections. And when I don't think I can take the feeling anymore, I explode with frustration. "I know, Aizel!" I wail, and Trond lets out an ear-splitting cry.

Sorcia and Aizel go silent so that the only sound in the cave is the crackling flames of the fire. I breathe deeply, steadying myself, relaxing myself, centering myself, so that the only voice I hear comes internally from Arik.

In that soft moment, we both hold our breath. The answer comes through loud and clear for we think it at the same exact time as if our minds have finally clicked together as one singular entity. And there's a voice. A voice from beyond the cave. From beyond the forest. A voice as sweet as berries. A voice that tempers my heightened rage.

Kill Grom.

Kill the Jarl.

Chapter Seven

In the Time of Darkness
In the Age of Ice
Wintertime, 666 AD
Caverns in the Far North
Night of the Waxing Crescent Moon

A collective gasp cuts its way through the cave like hot water searing through a block of ice. I know both Aizel and Sorcia heard the exchange between Arik and me.

"What?" Sorcia squeals. "No! You can't do that! I won't let you! I won't." She's in near hysterics, and her voice assaults my ears with such a deafening ring that I wince when it penetrates my head. Trond notices it too, for he cries out once more. I jostle him against my chest the way I'd seen Ylfa do with Trond to help calm him down.

"Why not, Sorcia? You know what this means. You know what this can do to our family. We must think about our own."

Sorcia sets her legs in a locked position and narrows her eyes. Her face tilts downward slightly so that the shadows from the fire dance about her face and create dark circles under her eyes. "You mean, your own," she snarls. Against the creamy white hue of her skin, it's alarming to look at—like she's been possessed with a foreign entity, a *draugr*. Only, I know she hasn't. This shift in demeanor comes from a deep place within her. A locked away place. A suppressed place. Her black eyes grow wide and wild, and for a split second, I am afraid. For a split second, with my precious baby brother tight against my chest, I am afraid. Of Sorcia. Of what she might do. Or try to do.

But only for a second.

Aizel puts two fingers in her mouth and creates a whistling sound that snaps us out of our stare-down.

"*Our* own," I say through gritted teeth.

"Of course," Sorcia says, dripping with sarcasm. "*Our* own."

I hug Trond closer to my body. "Sorcia, if you have something you want to say to me, why don't you just come out and say it?"

"Well, now that you bring it up, Blodwyn," she spits out, and the timbre of her voice is like a snake's hiss when she says my name. "I'm quite sour with you over the love spell."

My eyebrows raise. "Oh, you are, are you?"

"Yes. Quite cross, actually. It's as if you didn't want to perform it in the first place."

"I didn't," I flatly reply.

"Then why did you agree? Why even bother to do it with us if your heart wasn't there?" she pleads.

"Because you need three, Sorcia. You know that. And why would I deny you? If you have intent, and a goal, and want to try, why would I say no to you? Maybe if you didn't…" the volume of my voice climbs, and I stop myself mid-sentence.

"If I didn't what? Again, if I didn't go out on my own and…"

"Stop it!" Aizel yells. "This isn't what we need to focus on now! We all know what happened that night. Modir died that night! And that love spell had zero effect on Grom because it didn't work. Because they never work. One out of every hundred moontimes, Sorcia. You know the probability of the thing, so don't act surprised, or try to blame Blodwyn for not being committed to the cause. But Blodwyn, understand where her sorrow lies. She loves him. Even still, after his rejection of her, she loves him. And if there's any residual feelings you may have for him, or are trying to hurt her with them…"

I huff a contemptuous sigh. How dare she insinuate I still have feelings for Grom!

Sorcia's eyes soften and pool at the edges with genuine tears.

I relax my tense shoulders and look at her with a pained expression. "I'm sorry, Sister. There's no other way. If he tells the Jarl what I've done—what we've all done—you know what they'll do.

They'll come to our land, dig her up, and burn her on the pyre. I can't bring her back if she's a pile of ashes. And we can't bleed the world without her. Don't you want to live in paradise? Don't you want to bear witness to the great things my mother said we could accomplish? We can't cleanse it all and let the old ones through if she's not here. So, I need to try, and I need all of her in order for me—for *us*—to perform that ritual."

"But what if Grom didn't tell the Jarl, yet? What if he's waiting for him to get back from the raid?"

"Yes!" Aizel interjects. "We could do a glamour to hold Grom in silence."

I ponder the suggestion for a moment. "I suppose that could work. But there's only one way to find out. We'll go to Grom's and talk to him. Just talk. But if he doesn't tell us what we need to hear, then you know what we'll have to do."

Sorcia hangs her head low and sighs dramatically. "Fine," she relents. "You should have Arik give Trond back to Ylfa so we can go."

But when we look around the cave, Arik is nowhere in sight. He has already set out ahead of us to track the Jarl and his raiding party.

Concealed in the darkness, the three of us approach Grom's small pit house on the outskirts of the village. The structure is set about fifteen feet into the ground and has one access point of entry. As a single man with no family, he doesn't require much more than this. Had he and Sorcia committed themselves to being a married couple, they would have certainly moved to a larger dwelling—a longhouse, perhaps, where they would have eventually started a family. But that was not to be. For Grom had rejected Sorcia and her heksa ways, and I had one thing on my mind despite Sorcia's frantic pleas. *Kill Grom.*

"It should be me to confront him," Sorcia whispers.

"You really think that's a good idea?" Aizel asks. "I mean, I would assume he has some idea that you tried to bewitch him. Maybe he won't be as sympathetic to our plight."

"Well, who then?" she screeches, but her voice is but a raspy sigh. "You? Blodwyn?"

"No," I assert. "It should be you, Sorcia. But not you."

The two of them twist their faces in confusion.

"You know what to say, but he won't want to hear it from your mouth. You have the most experience with him, but he won't respond well to it coming from you. Take my face. Glamour me. He'll talk to me."

She sets her thin lips tightly together in a frigid scowl, then extends her hands to reach for mine and Aizel's. We form a circle in the snow outside the pit house and quietly begin the chant.

"Divine the image, the image is me. Give them the face I long to see," I say to start the spell.

"Blodwyn's face, the face of three. Perceive the image I long to see," Aizel says after.

"Blodwyn's face come unto me. Hers is the face I long to be," Sorcia concludes.

The wind rushes through our circle, and Aizel and Sorcia clench my hand tighter at the bite of the wind, but it bothers me not. I force my inner energy from the center of my chest and push it out through my arms and into them both, like my own flash of heat and power surging through them. When we open our eyes and disengage, there are two more of me in the circle. The *mes* smile and nod, and Sorcia-me tightens up the front of her cloak and knocks on the door. Aizel-me and I crouch down low in the snow out of the line of sight, undetected.

"Blodwyn?" Grom says in surprise when he opens the door. "What are you doing here?"

"Hello, Grom," she says, her voice perfectly matching my own.

"I wasn't expecting..."

"I know. May I come in? We need to talk."

"Sure, sure," he says and opens the door wider for her to enter. As soon as it's closed, Aizel-me and I creep closer to it and press our ears to the wood so we can hear what's transpiring within.

"What's going on?" he asks.

"I... I spoke with Sorcia. She told me that the two of you are no longer. I'm very sorry to hear of this. I know it must not be easy."

"I'm sorry, Blodwyn, but if you came here tonight to try to mend things between Sorcia and me..."

"No!" she interrupts. "No. I just..."

"Wait," he says with a questioning tone—an all-too-eager one, might I add. "Are you here to mend things between *you* and me?"

A long, condescending "tsk" escapes her mouth. "Ridiculous!" she scoffs, and I can only imagine the look of shame that overcomes his face. "I'm here about the Jarl. I've come to ask you not to tell him what Sorcia asked of you. Please, Grom. You loved my mother. After everything that happened between us, she was still good and kind to you and set you on your way. Please. For the respect of her and her memory, leave this alone," she begs.

"She's too much," Aizel-me says desperately. "That was too desperate!"

I bring a finger to my lips to silence her.

"I'm sorry, Blodwyn, but I've already told him."

Aizel-me's eyes go wide with fear. *And knowing.* Immediately, I switch on the inner eye in the center of my head and tune Arik into the conversation. If he's already out there tracking the Jarl, the next piece of information is going to be extremely vital.

"What do you mean?" Sorcia-me says in disbelief. I hear the *knowing* in her voice too, and it's rife with sadness and pain of the inevitable. "What did you tell him?"

"I told him what you did, Blodwyn. What you and your heksas did. I know what you plan to do. I'm not stupid. I grew up in your household. I know enough to know. And whatever your true intentions, well, it's wrong. It won't have anything but negative consequences. It's a bad path. The Jarl said that when he gets back from his raid, he will take care of it. Dig her up. Put her on the pyre proper, and then deal with you—you know there will be consequences for your dese-cration. Your magics and spells have gotten out of hand, Blodwyn. It needs to stop."

"How long do I have? Can you at least tell me that?" she pleads.

"The raid will go to the South End. Probably a month's time. Maybe less."

South End, I say in my mind's eye. I say to Arik. But for some inexplicable reason, I get the feeling that is where he is headed anyway. I hope he hears me though. Now that my visage and essence is split three ways, I fear the intensity and clarity of Arik's and my connection will somehow be diminished. His light isn't that bright in my head, and I wonder if Aizel-me and Sorcia-me are experiencing the flashing residuals.

"Grom, please. Is there anything I can say? Anything I can do? I would forever be in your debt if you told the Jarl when he got back that it was all a misunderstanding."

There's a shuffling sound from within the room. Movement. "What did you have in mind?" Grom says, and his voice has changed. Darkened. Taken on a sinister tone.

"Whatever pleases you," Sorcia-me answers.

Aizel stares at me—her gray eyes speak vol-umes. I raise my hand in the air, holding the both of us in position, poised to make a move into the pit house.

More shuffling sounds. Then squishing sounds. Sounds of deep and passionate kisses. Breathy moans from Sorcia-me. And I stop to think—*he* thinks he's kissing *me*! Does the same thought enter Sorcia's mind? Does it make her rage grow? Will the task at hand be easier to execute?

Then Grom lets out a long and subtle moan, and I know that's our signal to enter. I gently push on the door, and Aizel-me and I make our way into the front room. Grom stands, britches around his ankles, head tilted up to the ceiling, his long blond hair hanging heavily down his back. Sorcia-me kneels before him working her mouth furiously up and down his manhood. Quickly and quietly, Aizel-me and I flank him on both sides. The pleasure of Sorcia-me's mouth distracts him from the new presence in the room, but she's aware we've entered. She opens her eyes and winks at me to let me know we're moving forward with the plan.

"Enjoying this?" Aizel-me whispers in his one ear.

"Enjoying this?" I repeat in his other.

Startled by the double sound of my voice, Grom flinches and opens his eyes. He pulls back reflexively from Sorcia-me's mouth-grip, but she closes her jaw down harder on him and pulls him deeper into her mouth. He shudders as both the sensations of agony and ecstasy race throughout him at the same time. And when he looks to see not one, but *three* of me, he is visibly shaken and confused.

"W...w.... what?" he stammers. "How can this... How are you... What is going on here?"

Aizel-me runs her fingers through his long hair sending shivers down his back. "You don't need to understand," she purrs.

I mimic her actions and do the same. "You don't need to understand," I repeat.

He looks down at Sorcia-me's head bobbing up and down on his organ. She pulls him into her mouth with alternating quick and slow movements, then removes him completely and uses her tongue to lick him from base to tip. His eyes roll in the back of his head, and he moans, "This isn't real. This isn't happening."

"Oh, it's happening, all right," I say, and start kissing his earlobe and down his neck.

"Oh, it's happening, all right," Aizel-me says and does the same to him on his other side.

Sorcia-me stops moving and looks up at him, "Oh, it's definitely happening." She gives a coy smile and goes back to work on his manhood while the two of us continue to tantalize his other senses.

"Why do you bewitch me like this?" he whispers—to me, to Aizel, to Sorcia, to all of us and none of us at once. He speaks as if he's in a dream state—far away and distant, and quite possibly not in this world.

"Whatever do you mean?" Aizel-me says.

"Whatever do you mean?" I repeat.

"Whatever do you mean?" a third voice echoes, surprising all of us for it wasn't my voice from Sorcia-me. It was a voice calling from beyond the forest, racing through the wind. It was a dark and gravelly voice—hoarse and guttural. It was a voice from the great beyond, the great below, from the South End...

Arik.

I sigh to myself for I know he's reached his destination. He's tracked down the Jarl, and *he's* letting *me* know that everything is going to plan on his end of things.

I give Aizel a nod, and we clasp our hands behind Grom's back. The energy passing through us seems to light up the room.

"How can there be three of you," he moans. His eyebrows furrow leaving deep lines across his forehead. He struggles to hold back the release—to keep it in until the very last pleasurable second possible, to savor every moment of his organ in the depths of my mouth, my tongue lashing across every groove and ridge of him.

Is he remembering me? Is he imagining we're still together?

Suddenly, Sorcia-me stops and perks up. She eyes me coolly as if she read my mind.

Because she did.

And in one swift motion, she retrieves a blade from her back pocket—the same one she'd used to cut out the hare's heart, the same one she'd used to saw off her own locks, the same one she'd used to gash her palm open in the love ritual. The blade is still speckled with brown, dried blood as she'd never cleaned it all those months ago. With the sharp end, she slices down the length of a Grom's manhood. A thick, red line blooms up on the peach-colored skin, and he screams and bucks wildly from the pain. Immediately, Aizel-me and I each grab on to one of Grom's shoulders trying to lock him in place as he thrashes about. But then Sorcia-me takes his organ back into her mouth and continues sucking on him. The corners of her mouth ooze red with his blood mixed with her saliva.

He looks down at her and moans. Then screams. Then moans again. Then grimaces from the sting of his open wound on the most sensitive and pleasurable part of him. It must be so confusing for him. His mind and body not able to fully comprehend or discern between the delight and the anguish.

"What did you do? Why did you do that?" he cries out. "Stop! Stop! Please stop!" He tries to pull away, but between our physical grip and our astral one, he's unable to move.

Before long, his body tenses up—a clear indicator he's on the verge of ecstasy. He moans and groans and tries so desperately to escape us, but it's no use and he knows it. Sorcia-me pulls her head back at his supreme moment, and with the jerking motion of her head, she breaks the spell and is no longer under the mask of my visage. And as Grom's seed and blood combination spills onto the floor, Sorcia rises to meet him face to face. His icy blue eyes go wide with disbelief, and he stutters and stammers and tries yet again to break free of our hold. He whips his head side to side only to see me, the real Blodwyn, and Aizel.

"Witches! Witches! What have you done?" he screams. "What spell have you cast on me now?"

And with her lips stained with his fluid mixture, Sorcia kisses him deeply and violently, and he squirms at her touch. When she's finished, he spits and gags and curses our names. We three can't help but giggle at his unruly display.

"What have you done, Grom?" Sorcia says, taking her place in front of him. "You threaten our family? You betray the woman who was nothing but kind to you?"

A blinding flash jolts me from behind my eyes. Now that Sorcia and Aizel are no longer glamoured as me, I'm able to see the full vantage point of Arik in the South End. He's cornered the Jarl in the forest. They're alone.

The three of us join hands, and Grom's muscles tighten again. Fear has descended into his heart making him twist and turn with a sensation of utter hopelessness.

"Sorcia, please. Let me explain. Blodwyn, we can talk about this. Aizel, please, make them listen to you!"

"Sky above me," Aizel says.

"Earth below me," Sorcia says.

"Fire within me," I say.

"Sky above me."

"Earth below me."
"Fire within me."
"Sky."
"Earth."
"Fire."
"Sky."
"Earth."
"Fire."
"Fire."
"Fire."
"Fire."

We now say "Fire" simultaneously over and over again until the black runes on my arms glow orange. Until the scent of kindling fills the room. Until the smoke rises from the soles of Grom's feet. Through the burning light of the flames, South End comes into my vision as the Jarl's face melts away—his body pinned to a tree with a spear and his limp limbs turn to dust. I hear him scream once, then shock silences him. And through the burning light of the flames, Grom screams once as his body is engulfed in our sacred light.

I will rest easy tonight knowing my family is safe and that I can finally move forward with my plan to bring Modir back.

Chapter Eight

In the Time of Darkness
In the Age of Ice
Wintertime, 666 AD
Caverns in the Far North
Night of the Full Moon

The moon has risen thirteen times since Grom's incineration. Just enough time for us to gather the essentials, talk about the words to be said, and agree upon the invocations. This night of the full moon was our first real opportunity to attempt the resurrection, and we were ready. Quietly, the three of us witches crept into the back chamber where Ylfa spent most of her days doting over Trond. The glowing light of the torches within filters out into the long, rocky corridor. She's humming a song to the baby, one that's not familiar to my ears. I lead the way with Aizel and Sorcia right behind me.

"Ylfa? Ylfa?" I whisper at the archway to the opening of her room.

She doesn't hear me at first. Her attention steadfastly remains on the boy in her arms, and she swings him gently from side to side, continuing her mysterious lullaby.

"Ylfa," I say again, louder this time.

And again, she doesn't hear me. Or she *does* hear me, and she chooses to ignore me.

Sorcia pushes herself forward and into the chamber. "Oh, Ylfa!" she exclaims with a high-pitched, over-dramatic voice. "How are you, sister?"

Aizel and I follow her in.

Ylfa, unable to ignore the intrusion, clutches Trond tighter and looks up at us with her sullen, sunken eyes. Dark black circles round the edges of them and are contrasted sharply against her pale white face, a sure after-effect from not sleeping. Ylfa doesn't do much of anything these days but take care of Trond. Clean him, feed him, change him, feed him some more, rock him to sleep—the only thing of value in her life is to see him live his. Her attachment to him has clearly gone far beyond her need to have her child back.

Her attachment to him has gone dangerously too far.

It's obvious she hasn't been taking care of herself either. Her long blonde hair is twisted up in a loose bun at the top of her head, but the strands that shoot out at the sides are so oily they stick to the sides of her temples. Her clothes hang off her rail-thin frame. The only things left of her womanly shape are her engorged breasts from which she nurtures Trond. Other than that, she is frail. Sickly looking. Haggard. Her once lively eyes are empty, hollow, devoid of any life or spark. She cautiously gazes at us and mutters, "Oh... oh, hello? What do you three want?"

Her voice is shaky, unsteady, weak. Like she's about to break—like at any moment the sound of her own voice will crack her open from the inside out like an egg hatching.

And what will emerge from her broken body? *If I have it my way—Modir.*

Aizel copies Sorcia's attitude and approaches her. "Sweet Ylfa! Look at you! How long have you been with us now? Three full moons? And you've done nothing for yourself! You've been so focused on caring for the babe, you haven't stopped to consider *you*."

"Your wants," Sorcia sings. "Your needs."

"I... I... I'm fine," she stutters.

Sorcia and Aizel huddle around her and guide her to sit in the chair at the center of the room.

"Sweet Sister, you are not!" Aizel gushes. "Let us give you a reprieve for this night. Let us help you feel refreshed. Let us help you feel like you again."

They dance around her, and their voices combine into a lullaby, one *she* is unfamiliar with, and I see her vacant eyes get dizzy. "We'll wash your hair and brush it out," Sorcia says.

"Oh, yes!" Aizel claps her hands. "We'll give you proper braids. And get you out of these clothes and into fresh linens!"

It's all so innocuous on the surface—a group of friends coming to the aid of the despondent one in the group to pep her up and make her feel good again. But Ylfa is confused by their words and disoriented by their fluttering movements around her. With a swift hand, Sorcia takes a runestone and draws a circle on the stone floor, and Aizel sets the waxy candles at the appropriate direction points.

"But, Trond," Ylfa cries out with true anguish in her voice. She shifts the baby nervously at her chest and kisses the top of his head.

Finally, I step into the chamber, my arms extending at my sides. I clench both my hands, drawing all the air out of the room and into me, like taking a very deep breath. I am so over-filled with energy for that moment that it lifts me a few inches from the ground. Ylfa, Sorcia, and Aizel gasp for the breath I have stolen, and when I flick my hands open again, they sigh with relief. Sorcia doesn't appreciate that trick. I can tell. She gives me a quick sideways glance that wasn't really meant for me to see. But I did. And I'm taking note. I approach Ylfa in the chair, and without saying a word, peel Trond from her arms and walk out. She barely has a chance to protest because she is dazed—perplexed by the double-talk of my companions. They use their words to distract, and their bodies to divert from what is truly taking place.

I take Trond and head back to the main vestibule. "No child should be without their mother," I say to him, and he stares up at me with his magic gray eyes. My breath catches in my throat as they flash at me—gray to silver to gold. And

I think—*She's in there. Modir is in there.* A spark
of her is locked away in his eyes—the last gift
she bestowed upon him. "Don't you worry, Baby
Brother. I will bring her back, for I can tell you all
the stories and relay to you all my memories of
her, and it still wouldn't be enough. I will bring
her back so you can make your own memories
and have your own stories to pass down the line."

He feels light as air. Weightless. Like he's not
a person of this world but rather an astral being
sent from the old ones. And his scent intoxicates
me—fills me with a newness and freshness and…
Purpose.

Arik waits for me by the altar where we make
the exchange—I hand him the child, and he
hands me a satchel filled with dirt—the dirt from
Modir's grave, the dirt that I will use to summon
her from the clutches of the old ones. By not putting her body to the pyre, Modir's spirit can still
travel between the realms and find solace in her
once corporeal form. But only for a moment. And
if I can catch that moment correctly and call her
back while she's in there, then I can displace Ylfa's
spirit, trap it in Modir's corpse, and have Modir's
lifeforce take root in Ylfa. Once she's back, Modir
can nurse her baby boy like she was meant to, and
I can embrace her once again, seek her counsel,
and help her lead us to the ultimate paradise. For
she is the one, true Blodheksa. Now and forever.

"Thank you," I say.

He nods and grunts.

"Are you sure you'll allow me to do this? To Ylfa? You know what it means if I can transfer the spirit. Ylfa will be trapped there. She will probably be aware of what is happening."

He nods again.

"Speak now, Arik. Last chance. Sorcia and Aizel are ready for me. I was just waiting on the burial dirt from you, and…"

"No child should be without their mother," he says in a low voice.

He heard me.

But I'm not surprised. He always hears me. I could stop the flow of astral thoughts if I wanted to, but I don't want to. There's something comforting with Arik in my head. Like I'm never alone.

This time I nod at him reverently. I could only imagine how difficult it must have been for him—to see the woman he loved so deeply descend into a shell of her former self. He didn't really see it though, did he? He had been ravaged with partial blindness long before they lost their daughter. He didn't necessarily witness the decline, but he was more than aware of the madness that infected her mind. To him, Ylfa has been dead for some time now. To him, I am his light, and his way, and his new life. And if experimenting on Ylfa—if using her body to summon my mother back from the beyond is going to advance our common goal of a new world, he'll allow it.

I touch Trond's back one last time and turn to go back to the alcove.

Chapter Eight

When I return to the room, Aizel and Sorcia are milling about Ylfa with swift and wild gesticulations. Aizel bounces around the room lighting torches and lining up the tools for the ceremony at the rock ledge by Ylfa's bed. She waves her arms around frantically leaving vision trails behind her like some crazed fever dream. Ylfa is entranced. She slumps forward, naked in the chair, her shoulders hunched over and her head practically in her lap. Between Aizel's motions and Sorcia's singing, poor Ylfa is completely out of sorts.

Sorcia pops her head up from behind Ylfa when I enter and approach them. "Arik has Trond?" she asks.

I nod.

"Her hair is washed. I'm just finishing the braid."

"Was Modir's hair long enough?" I ask.

"Every last inch!" she exclaims.

I saunter over and inspect Sorcia's handiwork, and just as she said, strands of my mother's hair are intricately woven into Ylfa's new fresh, tight braid. "Good," I approve.

"She's washed and clean, too," Aizel adds.

I nod again, saving my words for the ceremony, and open the satchel and dig a hand deep into the cold dirt within. I roll every grain, every particle in between my fingers before taking a handful and spreading it out in the shape of a star inside the circle Aizel previously made around Ylfa in her chair.

"How are you, Ylfa? Aizel and Sorcia taking care of you?" I sing in a high-pitched voice.

Aizel scrunches her nose. "Valerian. She's sedated."

"Good," I respond. "Do you have the cup?"

"Right here," Aizel says.

"And the blade?"

"Here," Sorcia says. She bounces into the circle with us and hands me her dagger. It's still unclean—specks of brown and clumps of gore adorn the metal and the hilt, but this is good. This is the way I need it to be for the ritual.

"Let's begin, shall we," I say and look to Aizel to start the rite. The three of us disrobe and stand naked in the circle, each at a point in the star.

Aizel lifts the silver chalice with one hand. She pours the fruit wine into it and passes it to me. I run the sharp edge of Sorcia's blade across my palm and squeeze my hand into the fruit wine. Back and forth, round and round, I twirl the chalice so that my blood incorporates with the liquid therein. I place the blade in the circle, walk over to Ylfa, and kneel before her. The underside of my heavy breasts rests on her knees. Her skin is so cold against my heat, but she doesn't notice my skin touching hers. "Ylfa," I whisper gently. "Sit up for me, dear. Let me have a look at you. Let me see how the girls have taken care of you. Let me see how well you've been taking care of Trond."

With lazy, half-opened eyes, she looks up at me. Her pupils are round and large—the blackness of them obliterates their usual ice-blue color. "Trond?" she lazily asks. "Is he well?"

"Oh, yes. Nothing to worry about. He just needs a little sip. To calm him down. Will you allow me to…"

Ylfa musters up all the energy left in her soul and tries to sit up at attention. She pushes her shoulders back so that the fullness of her breasts extends up and out. Gently, I grip one of her nipples between my fingers and squeeze. The hazy white liquid bubbles to the surface, and I catch one, two, three drops of the sustenance in the cup and swish it around some more. "Thank you, Mother," I say and hoist myself up to stand.

"Was that enough?" she asks with a concerned voice, a hollow and desperate plea.

"Quite enough, yes," I reassure, and she smiles and slumps back down into her hunched position.

"For thou who sleeps in stone and clay!" I raise the cup in the air, take a drink, and pass it to Aizel.

"Rise up and obey," she says, drinks, and passes to Sorcia.

"Journey back through the Mortal door," Sorcia says, drinks, and passes the cup back to me.

"Assemble flesh, and walk once more," I say and finish the mixture. "Modir, heed this call."

We begin to chant. Sway. A song plays in our heads—a collective song that the three of us hear. A drum in the distance getting louder and louder. A humming from beyond rising to a discordant song—one with no rhyme or reason, or meter or measure, or harmony or melody, just sound—pure and grating on our collective ears. And underneath the chaotic din is the beauty of the music—its rawness, its realness, its frenetic energy that isn't really music at all, but *is*. I feel so limited in this human coil to not have the right words to explain how it sounds, or more importantly, how it feels. But I do know, whatever it is, it raises the three of us up from the stone ground and makes my arms tingle with wavy pulses rippling underneath the surface of my tattooed flesh.

In the ancient tongue, in the long-lost language, Aizel speaks the words. And I speak the words. And Sorcia speaks the words. But there is no translation for them, for they just *are*. To the human ear and mind, it is nothing but drivel and babble, but to us it is life, and power, and light, and control. And we call to her—to Modir. We call to the old ones to set her free and sanction her return. *For yours is the kingdom, and the power, and the glory, now and forever.*

Ylfa stirs. She shifts her position, crossing one leg over the other. A quiet moan escapes her lips, and I open my mouth to continue the chant, but a searing pain takes over my abdomen and I stumble forward a step. Aizel and Sorcia look at me with worry. I compose myself and try again, but another wave of pain brings me to my hands and knees at Ylfa's feet.

"Blodwyn!" Aizel cries.

"Don't... stop..." I stammer, but they've stopped. They rush to my side to come to my aid, and I want to kill them both for breaking the circle, for not pushing on.

But I can't ignore the pain—this burning ache all throughout the lower half of my body and a surge of pressure from between my legs. I shimmy myself onto my backside and bend my legs and hold on tightly to my knees. I lose control of my insides, and urine sprays into the circle. I cry out in agony from the pressure and the pain.

"Blodwyn! What is happening?" Sorcia says as she gathers my white braids over my shoulder.

"I don't know! I don't know!" I scream, rocked by another wave of pain. My arms burn. My brands glow orange and a line of sweat forms on Sorcia's forehead from just being close to me.

Aizel presses on my stomach, and I howl from her touch. She then separates my legs slightly and examines my sacred area. My sex burns. The crevice between my legs is hot. On fire.

"Something's coming," Aizel says, trying to maintain her composure.

"What do you mean, something's coming!" I scream.

"Did you lie with Arik, Blodwyn?" she asks me calmly.

Sorcia touches my stomach, and I smack her hand away. "Yes! Yes!" I cry out.

"Are you with child?" Aizel asks like I've heard her ask so many other women in our village.

"No! That's impossible. I can't be! He didn't..."

Heat radiates all over my chest and up my neck. I burn. I burn. I'm burning. I'm burning. I scream again, the sound of my voice carries through the entire cave. Arik heads for the chamber with Trond in hand, but I yell "No! Don't!" out loud and in my head, stopping him in his tracks.

"Well, get ready, Sister, because something is coming," Aizel repeats. "I think you're going to have to push... right... about... now..."

I squeeze onto Sorcia's hand, my face scrunches up, and I give one deep and hard push.

"Oh my! What is that? What is happening?" Sorcia exclaims.

Something slithers its way out from my lower abdomen and between my legs. Slithers out of my sex, taking the burning and pain and pressure with it. Like a small white worm, the serpent is born and slinks up my thigh, wiping itself on my flesh, cleaning itself of the blood and fluids and gore, and warming itself on the heat of my skin.

Mesmerized by the creature, I notice new brands emblazoned on the front of my chest— more runes that have burned themselves up my neck and under my chin, and on the front area stopping right where my breasts begin.

"Blodwyn," Aizel remarks, "I don't think you are the Blodheksa."

"I told you I wasn't," I say, breathlessly.

"Then, what are you?" Sorcia asks.

I shrug my shoulders, but my gaze is fixed on the baby viper at my thigh. My sweet white serpent. My own special creation.

"I don't know exactly what's happening right now," Aizel says, "but one thing is for sure, you're transcending, Blodwyn. Your power is expanding exponentially, and I will need to examine your new markings soon."

"Later. Later. Let me rest."

"Of course," Sorcia says and leaves my side.

"Ylfa?" I ask.

"Still Ylfa," Sorcia says.

I extend my arm to my serpent. It wiggles up my warm flesh and coils its body around my bicep. "It's fine. For now," I say and stare, mystified, into her pearly pink eyes.

Chapter Nine

In the Time of Darkness
In the Age of Ice
Summertime, 673 AD
Caverns in the Far North
Afternoon of the Waxing Gibbous Moon

The scent of the burning incense wafts throughout the vestibule—it's a hearty smell that fills the space with thick smoke. It reminds me of a summer sunset when the sky is a dome of gradient colors stemming upward from the edge of the horizon with its yellows and oranges, reds and purples, and blues and blacks. The edge of the horizon. The edge of the world. Only it's just this human world that has edges. My new world will be free of the construct of human existence, and there will be no space or time. In my new world, when I rip the seams of the sky wide open, there will be no limitations to my power and the power of the old ones as they tumble forward and take back what was once theirs!

I hum out loud, and Aizel walks quickly around the circle with a finger to her lips to quiet me down. I know it's the incense—the incense that lulls me in and out of consciousness, in and out of reality, between this world and the next. Aizel had spent days preparing the incense. She concocted the special blend of herbs and plants and perfumes, and it is just the right combination to alter my state of mind. I am at peace. I am calm. I allow myself to be swept away in the delicious smells of the cave. My focus isn't really focus at all. But that's the point—to be here, but not.

Because I'm here—physically. My naked body rests on top of a layer of dirt within the sacred circle. Dirt from Modir's grave. But in my mind, I'm not here. I'm dancing wild in the sky with the fire of my brethren. I'm floating on top of the water in the open sea. And I'm with Arik in the back room outlining Ylfa's naked body with bronze sewing needles. Each one pierces her skin and brings a tiny red bubble to the surface. Like a studded goddess, the light from the torches around her glints off her metal barbs creating a spikey glow in the cave. Every puncture opens her up and releases slivers of her soul. Spindly smoke trails rise from every opening and gather around her head like a ghostly crown. *A hundred doorways.* Ylfa's head bobs back and forth in time with the music that fills her head—music that I put there seven sun cycles ago when I first took control over her body. Aizel doesn't need to use the Valerian root anymore as Ylfa has been in a permanent state of sedation since Trond was weaned off her breast. I trapped her in her own mind with my song that plays a constant loop of her favorite memories—confined her in a constant daydream of peaceful bliss.

A thumping sound of a heartbeat grows louder in my ear, and the serpent on my stomach raises her head at attention for she hears it too.

"Relax, Blodwyn," Aizel coaxes. "When you two squirm around like that, it makes it hard for me to read you."

I breathe in. The air fills my lungs sharply, but I exhale in such a calculated and measured way that I am able to settle myself down.

Relax.

The serpent rests on my skin again as Arik places the last needle into Ylfa. She mumbles something, but I'm so hazy I can't hear what she says. Aizel's eyes widen in shock and despair, and an unintentional gasp leaves her lips.

"What?" I inquire, alarmed.

She furrows her brow, and in my mind, Arik begins removing the needles from Ylfa.

"Wait!" I cry out. "What is he doing?"

"What is *who* doing?" Aizel responds, trying to remain calm. But it's no use, anxiety is heavily wrought upon her face.

I sit up and the serpent slinks away from my body, out of the circle, and over to her nesting place at the altar. "Arik! He's removing the needles from Ylfa! It took him so long to adorn her, and he's just... just... giving up?"

"Blodwyn, sit still!" Aizel forcefully commands.

Chapter Nine

The room tilts and spins, and it feels as if the ground beneath me is opening to swallow me alive. But I'm frozen at Aizel's command, and my reptile companion has left the circle, and my guardian lover is breaking the ritual and wiping the blood dots from Ylfa's body, and my tattoos are so very, very hot that I don't think I can contain the heat emanating from them and...

"Wait! Blodwyn! Get up!" Aizel screams, snapping me out of my semi-hallucination. My mind wrestles with her first command to stay still and her new command of rise, but I soon realize that the grave dirt is smoldering from my heat. Quickly, I jump up and over the runestones surrounding the star.

"What happened?" I implore, my trance now broken and the full capacity of my faculties back intact. "What's going on?"

Aizel sighs, exasperated. "I... I don't know."

I shake my head from side to side and a puff of dirt billows around me. "I don't know what else to do! I'm running out of ideas here! I don't understand why everything I try ends up failing."

Aizel scurries over to the altar and scribbles down runes on the wooden surface.

"What are you writing?"

"It changed. It all changed. The variations have been consistent over the years—enough for me to commit to memory. But now? Whatever happened just now changed the entire landscape of *you*."

My runes. She speaks of the words emblazoned on my body—the magic story gifted to me by my mother. Aizel has spent the last seven years reading me, committing them to memory, and deciphering the meaning of all of it. Seven long and arduous years of endless nights chanting and humming and analyzing and evaluating. All for naught, so it seems.

"What do you mean, they changed?"

She throws a hand up at the side of her face and continues to furiously dig the sharpened bone into the tabletop. She makes deep and deliberate indentations so as to not forget what she has temporarily saved in her mind.

"Aizel!" I plead. "Tell me!"

"Like I said, every once in a while, mostly after a ritual, your brands ... shift. Normally, a word here or there and sometimes a sentence or two. But the meaning has always been the same. Like the same story being told over and over by different people—the way it's told might be different, the words used might be different, but the overall tone and message of it all stays the same. That's what brings life to tales. The breath that speaks the words breathes life into the story making it real and palpable."

"And you're saying you noticed something turn on me?"

"Turn. Shifted. Changed. Whatever you want to call it. There are whole new passages adorning you now. It's like the second part of a living spell. You are the word, Blodwyn."

"But what does it mean? Does it have anything to do with what Arik did? How he stopped his end of the ritual without warning. And more importantly, why did this happen?"

She stops writing on the altar, pulls her red hair up into a twisted, messy bun, and spins on her heel to face me. "Think of every other spell you've done—*we've* done—other than love spells, our measure of success is high. But this? This seems to be the one ritual none of us can get right. I know you don't want to entertain the idea, but what if you really are the Blodheksa, and Modir is just a guide? What if the Blodheksa is supposed to be marked in the same manner that you are? What if we're not supposed to bring Modir back? Could that be why every attempt has failed?"

Her words grate on my every nerve, and I instinctually clench a fist in the wake of my rising anger and annoyance. "What do the new runes say?" I ask through gritted teeth.

"Hear my words, Blodwyn. What if Arik is your conduit? The way your father was to your mother?"

"What do the new runes say?" I ask again, my voice raising in volume a little.

"I don't mean to sound like Sorcia, but what if…"

"What do the new runes say?" I yell, cutting her off.

She breathes in quickly and deeply, my anger giving her pause. "I'm not sure," she says, eyes trained on the floor. "I'll have to get a closer look."

She's lying. She doesn't do it often, but I always know when she does. I can't quite figure out if she's lying to protect me from something or someone or, even, myself, but she's lying all the same. I dismiss her subterfuge this once because I know she is only trying to help me. She has been loyal to me our whole lives, so there must be a good reason for her deception. The funny thing is she knows I know she's lying. Her cheeks flush pink for a second with hot embarrassment.

"Impossible," I growl.

"What? What's impossible?"

"It's impossible that Arik is my conduit."

"Why do you say that?"

"Because I lay with him, Aizel. Often. Regularly. For seven years now. And not once

have I been blessed with the twins. I bore only the serpent after I laid with the serpent. But a child? Children? It's not meant to be. And I know it feels like forever since we've had a Blodheksa to guide us, but I promise you, she is here. I know Sorcia would say that…"

Something in Aizel's expression shifts and causes me to pause my words. Her golden eyes cycle through every color imaginable like a rainbow wheel spinning around in her brain. The sides of her mouth drop down into a frown, and she furrows her eyebrows so tightly together it looks like one thin line of red wispy hair runs across her forehead.

"Sorcia," she says slowly, quietly.

"What about her? She took Trond out so we could do the ritual. Do you think it failed because she wasn't here?"

"Sorcia," she repeats, ignoring my comment.

"What Aizel? What about her?"

"Blodwyn, you and I both know that since we killed Grom and the Jarl, Sorcia has been a little distant. Rightly so."

"I don't know if I would say distant. I know she had her anguish towards me for what we did, but I'm sure she's gotten over it. I mean, it *has* been seven years."

"But Blodwyn, what if she hasn't! Since Grom, she's been weaving in and out of relationships, always trying to find her 'one,' as she says. But what if it's not really a relationship she's looking for…"

"What if it's a conduit…" I whisper.

"Exactly. How many men has she entertained since Grom?"

"Countless!" I huff in a joking way, but after the words leave my lips and reach my own ears I soon question how much of a joke it really is.

"Exactly! What if her intention is to bear the twins and declare herself the Blodheksa? What if that has been her intention all along?"

"Shhhhh," I say, pressing my hand to her mouth. "Speak not such words of our sister." *Besides, she'll be returning with the boy soon*, I say directly into her mind. "I don't think Sorcia would do or think anything like that. She's been faithful to us. Good to us. Has she not been helping us in the cause?"

Aizel pulls away from my grasp. "No. No. You're right," she relents.

"Speak of it no more," I command, but it's too late. The damage is done. The thought has entered my brain, and I can already feel it starting to take root and fester there. It makes the markings on my skin tingle and itch.

Arik appears in the vestibule with a twine basket filled with the sewing needles he removed from Ylfa's body. The pained expression on his face brings me back to the sad reality that I have failed yet again. "It's alright," I want to say to him, but the words never make it out, nor do they inject themselves into his mind in our astral language. Because it's not alright. It's frustrating and depressing and irritating. I manage a "thank you" instead.

He nods at me forlornly and puts the basket on the altar. "I think Aizel Is right."

I glare hard at him. Arik has always been a man of few words, and when he did speak, it was usually something worth listening to. His confirmation of sharing Aizel's suspicions adds a layer of uneasiness to my already anxious mind. My skin itches again, and I rotate my shoulders to spin the feeling away. "What did Ylfa say to you that made you stop the ceremony?" I ask, changing the subject.

"They're coming."

"Who's coming?" Aizel asks. "Sorcia and Trond?"

He shakes his head. "I sensed it was someone else. Someone not from here. *Something* else."

"Why didn't I sense it?" I ask.

"You were in the circle, Blodwyn. The incense."

I nod. "Could it be an entity? A draugr?"

"Nothing like that. Ships from faraway shores," Arik says. "Ships from the otherlands. That was the impression I got."

Aizel paces the floor. Each step is slow and thoughtful as if she's formulating many thoughts with every movement. She runs both hands up the sides of her face and gathers her hair in a reckless bun at the top of her head. *Collecting her thoughts.* Gathering them and piecing them together one by one.

"What are we thinking, Aizel?" I prod after she's walked around me a few times.

"Ships from the faraway shores," she repeats Arik's words. "I don't know, but this could be something."

"What could be something?" I inquire.

"The Jarl of Frostheim," she begins, "the one Arik pursued. His son took over for him after he went missing on his raid."

"He was but a boy of fourteen at the time. He has no real power. The Council handles things in his name until he comes of age," I say.

"He's of age now, isn't he? He'll be the official Jarl, and the Council's power will be diminished soon."

"Soon," Arik adds.

"Very soon," she reiterates. "It's no secret this Council and new Jarl are interested in exploring the otherlands. Over the years, they've had peaceful envoys traveling both ways, learning our tongues, trading goods, and exchanging practices and traditions. The Council and the Jarl are said to be very forward-thinking and are open to new ideas and customs." The sudden lilt in her voice embarrasses me, for all this time has passed and my knowledge of politics and the happenings of my own village hasn't been of my concern. Modir, Trond, Arik—those were the source of my focus. I couldn't care less about the boy-Jarl and his over-bearing Council. But suddenly, I'm ashamed of my ignorance of the topic.

My cheeks get hot, so I click my tongue on the roof of my mouth to hide my shame. "For what reason?"

"Expansion? Conquest, perhaps? To know thine enemy…" she surmises.

I huff with annoyance. "Do they not know the possible consequences of opening such doors?"

"Are they really any different from the doors we're trying to open?" Aizel retorts.

"You know what I mean. Ours is not to be compared. They are men. Men are vile and weak and know not their potential or their limitations. We are not men. We are gods, Aizel."

"Understood," she answers. "Maybe these ships from the otherlands means there will be people here for the Jarl's official presentation?"

"They've been gathering at the shoreline. Setting up camp," Arik says. "Little by little."

"Infiltrating our land?" I ask.

"Little by little," Aizel repeats.

"And that's mainly where Sorcia spends her days, right?" I ask.

"By the village shoreline. Yes."

And as if she had been listening to our entire conversation, Sorcia saunters in with Trond gripping her hand. My hand quickly darts between my legs to conceal my nakedness from my brother's eyes. Sorcia looks about the room surveying the ritual scene and the wide grin on her face quickly melts away to a downward frown. "It didn't work again," she pouts, but her emphasis on the word "again" fills me with a burst of rage.

Trond releases her hold and outstretches his arms to me. "Blodwyn! Blodwyn!" he calls, but his lips are sewn together with thick, black thread, and his eyes are bulges of raw, pink flesh with the lids swollen shut and protruding from his face.

I blink.

"That's too bad," Sorcia says, extending her lower lip. Blood pours out from the inside of her mouth and gathers in a pool at her feet.

I blink again to shake myself of the sight, and a hollow wave washes through my body—a sinking feeling that makes me dizzy and weak. Arik blinks too, and we synchronize our eyes until the premonition slowly fades away each time they open and close. I realize Sorcia and Trond are not here.

"Wait!" Aizel exclaims. "What was...?"

"You saw them, too?" I ask her frantically.

She nods, and I grip Arik's arm, nervously tugging at his coat. "We have to find them!"

"She'll be in the village by the lake," Aizel urges.

"Stay here in case they come back," I command and lead Arik out of the cave.

Chapter Ten

In the Time of Darkness
In the Age of Ice
Summertime, 673 AD
Village on the Outskirts of the Frostheim Forest
in the Far Northlands
Evening of the Waxing Gibbous Moon

A rik and I wasted no time making our way to the village. He tried his best to keep me calm, but I know he saw the same vision as I did—Trond's mutilated face and Sorcia's blood-filled mouth. I know he felt the same foreboding and ominous feeling in the pit of his stomach—the icy grip of the hand of fear. Keeping me calm was an impossibility.

My mind immediately told me Trond was in danger, and Sorcia was either the one putting him in harm's way or she was unable to protect him from whatever the threat was. That part was unclear, so with my nose to the sky like a she-wolf, I sniffed the air, trying to pick up on Trond's scent or Sorcia's, whoever I got wind of first. Connected, Arik and I use our double vision to sense any aura trails our kin left behind—because Arik saw in brilliant and colorful light, he was able to see the remnants of a person's soul when they walked about. He had said mine was red, Aizel was yellow, Sorcia blue, Trond white, so between the two of us we used our preternatural abilities to hunt, locate, and retrieve.

It had been a long while since I had been among the members of the community, and I take note of how much has changed. Years ago, people from the otherlands sent groups of their religious order over to our shores under the protection of the Jarl. Their purpose was to educate us in their ways and to make us a more worldly society considering we were cut off from the rest of the population by ice and snow. There were elders in our village who refused to believe there was land and culture that stretched beyond our frozen barricades. So, when the Jarl allowed these emissaries into our town, they had been met with much resistance from our native people. But that Jarl was dead, and a new one was in his place, and years had turned into understanding and acceptance and empathy, and more missionaries were being shipped over. They brought with them tools and clothes and food and steel all in exchange for a gathering here and some preaching there. What had started as a small tent city of a handful of these missionary people had now grown into a new development with pit houses under construction for a more permanent stay and people who looked like us, but were not us, milling about the lakeside property.

"The Jarl invited them," Arik says, sensing my displeasure at the outlanders.

"Hmmmm," I snarl with disgust.

Arik stops in his tracks and points to one of the completed pit houses. "Trond," he says.

I close my eyes and breathe in heavily. A sweet smell fills my nose. It's subtle, but I know it's there—just underneath the smell of burning wood and meat, the smell of toil and steel work, the smell of the open village and all those who dwell in it.

Trond.

I waste no time, sprint to the arched door, and enter unannounced. A group of five people sit in a circle on the floor. Their heads snap in my direction as fear overcomes their faces at my disruption. A man in a chair at the head of the circle looks up at me with large brown eyes and smiles. Sorcia jumps up from the circle in shock. "Blodwyn?" she croaks. "What are you doing here?"

"Was that you beckoning to me?" I yell at her. "What did you do? Where's Trond?"

Her eyes go wide. She's speechless. She knows not what I mean.

"Blodwyn?" a sweet voice calls from the circle. "You came?" Trond races over and grips me in a tight embrace.

Frantically, I disengage from his hold, kneel before him, and push his white hair back from his forehead. I furrow my brow as I twist and turn his face in each direction inspecting his mouth, his eyes, his ears. I cup his chin in my hands. "Are you hurt? Are you sick? What happened? What's going on here?"

Trond squirms away and crinkles his nose. "What's wrong with you?" he whines. "I'm fine. I'm fine!"

I stand up again and pull him close to me, the top of his head touching the bone of my hip. For a child of seven, he's above average height. Furiously, I rub his hair and back. "We're going, Sorcia. Now." I command.

A look of pleading enters her eyes, begging me to stay, begging me not to make a scene and call her away from whatever was going on in the pit house. The man in the chair stands up and approaches. I protectively tighten my grip on Trond.

"Wait, Blodwyn," Sorcia begins, "let me introduce you to Michael. Michael this is Blodwyn, the one I told you about."

The one called Michael takes a step closer. But it's a cautious step. I can see the trepidation practically ooze out of him. There's a level of fear, curiosity, and wonder in his gestures.

"He speaks our tongue?" I whisper from the side of my mouth.

"The common tongue, yes," she replies.

"Blodwyn, the Marked," Michael sings. His words I understand, but his accent jars me— grates on my ears. "I've heard so much about you." A smile spreads across his face as if time has slowed down. It's an eerie smile that I find unsettling.

With one hand, I push Trond's shoulder and force him to get behind me. I turn my attention back to Michael. "That's interesting as this is the first time I'm hearing about you."

Michael's eyes smile at me. They're big and round and a deep shade of brown like the bark of an ash tree. There's a gentleness in his demeanor, an innocence that I can't deduce whether it's feigned or real. Maybe I've been suspicious of people for far too long and I can no longer tell genuine goodness from pretended intentions. He laughs and the sound encircles him in blue, fragmented light. Sorcia-blue. My arms start to pulsate, and I look behind me to Arik. "Take him," I say. "Go." Quickly, Arik reaches for the boy, and with one hand, he grabs onto Trond's arm. With the other, he grips the handle of his blade at his waistband. As they slowly walk backward outside, Arik never once takes his eyes off Michael.

"Come. Sit. Share a cup," Michael beams and gestures for me to join the circle of his congregation.

I narrow my eyes at Sorcia, but her eager reaction tells me all I need to know. She so desperately wants me to sit and join their little group. She so desperately wants me to converse with this Michael person. *She so desperately wants my approval.* I send my thoughts to her mind — thoughts that scream *Why do you need the approval of a man to validate you?* Her shoulders stiffen a little, and I raise my hand to bid her relax. I nod at Michael, accepting his offer, and sit down at the edge of the circle on the floor. Sorcia joins me, and Michael instructs one of the others in the circle to bring me a cup of wine. One of the tenets of our culture was deeply rooted in hospitality laws. As a guest in his home, Michael would need to seriously think twice about bringing harm to me for fear of harsh reprisal.

"Drink this, and be welcome in my home," he says, handing me the cup.

I take a swig and grimace.

"What? No good?" he asks.

"Your wine is stale. Tastes like death."

Sorcia nudges me with her elbow in embarrassment.

Michael smiles. "You know what death tastes like, Blodwyn?" he asks, and there's a suspicious, almost condescending tone in his voice. I wonder just how much Sorcia has told him about me — about us, about our family, about our way of life.

I glare at him as I chug the last of it. Red lines of the liquid escape the sides of my mouth and dribble down my chin. With a final swallow and an "Ahhh," I proceed to wipe my face with the back of my hand. The people around me stir with disgust and rumble their admonitions — the uncivilized woman in *their* circle. Heavens forbid! "Mine is better," I sneer.

"Well, I'll have to try it sometime," he muses, but his gaze turns away from me and focuses on Sorcia. Her face lights up when he acknowledges her.

"Michael and the group are doing great things for Frostheim," Sorcia announces.

"Oh," I say. "Tell me, Michael, what is it you and your group do here? It's been a while since I visited the village. The last time I was here, your assembly was small and made camp in tents. There was barely a handful back then. You've grown some, haven't you?"

Michael inhales and takes his seat again at the head of the circle. The wall behind him is decorated with crosses and small paintings—iconography for some unfamiliar practice. "Your Jarl is kind and generous, and he's interested in what's beyond your borders. We learned your language, and because of that, we've been able to bridge certain gaps and bring our cultures together."

"Yes, yes. Bridge gaps," I repeat, flustered. "You seem to have mastered our tongue. But your native accent still rings true."

He chuckles. "Ahhh, yes. Bad habits are hard to break. I guess it makes us feel like we still have a piece of home in us." The others in the group chuckle too. But nothing he said was funny or amusing, and I know it's the laughter of nerves. Michael is their leader, and they take their cues from him. If he sighs, they sigh. If he laughs, they laugh. If he drinks, they drink. I scarcely think they even know why they behave the way they do. It's all in service to him, their guide, their shepherd, their… *conduit*?

Sorcia's eyes flash. She quickly looks from Michael to me, back to Michael, then to me again. And as I watch her watching him, it hits me — with his dark hair and dark eyes, he looks like a true outsider. *Like her.* She came to us as a stray from the nomadic tribes with black hair like crow feathers and piercing black eyes beaming like the night sky. Has Sorcia found a kindred spirit? Is that why her starry eyes glow at the sound of his voice?

"But really," I press, "what is the larger calling? It must be something important because you've not only planted yourselves in a more permanent fashion here on the lakeside, but you've certainly garnered the favor of one of my most trusted companions."

Another elbow to my side as Sorcia's pale cheeks turn bright red.

Michael clasps his hands together and places them on top of his knees. "To preach the word of God, of course! It is our goal, our mission, to touch as many lives as we can — to spread the good news about our Lord and Savior, Jesus Christ."

"Amen," one of the congregation members calls out, and the rest of them respond, "Amen."

Sorcia included.

The fire underneath my skin flares red for a second as the anger grips the back of my throat with acidy bile.

"Have you heard the good news, Blodwyn? Have the stories of the Lord made their way to your cave?"

Chapter Ten

I stand up and reach my arm out bidding Sorcia to rise with me. Hesitantly, she takes my hand, and I help hoist her up. "I can't say that they have."

"Well," he sighs, "when Sarah is ready, I'm sure she'll share with you everything she has learned from us."

Sorcia's face blooms pink again. "I'm sure she will," I say through gritted teeth.

"Or maybe I can make the trip to you? We can talk about life in general, our goals and aspirations, faith. We can even indulge in some of that wine you speak so highly of." He gives me a wink, and I shake my head to rid myself of the image.

I tug on Sorcia's hand, dragging her to the door. "Thank you," I say. "I'll take that under advisement."

We're barely out of the house when I explode on her. I squeeze her hand as tight as I can and do everything in my power to temper myself enough to not kill her. Because a flash inside of me wants her dead. Now. Every emotion from sadness to betrayal plays like gentle notes of a larger song in my body, and the tattoos at my throat sting like a thousand bites of a garden spider. It's a struggle to level out my breathing—like pulling hard on my internal reigns to calm me down.

Temper, temper, brings the tempest, a voice says my mother's words in my head, but it's not my mother's voice who says them. It's a dark voice, like steel scraping against gravel a hundred miles away, but ringing out to only me in the dusky evening. The corner of my eye catches the sight of Arik and Trond approaching us from the side of Michael's home.

"You're going to have to explain yourself, Sorcia. And fast!" I scream as I drag her away from Michael's house and onto the main dirt road. Arik and Trond had been waiting on the side of the house and followed us when we exited.

She stumbles over her own feet, and I can't help but wish for her to fall face first onto the side of the street.

"Wait, Blodwyn," she starts, reaching her arm out for me to help her.

I ignore the gesture. "I don't want you ever bringing Trond back there, do you understand? How long have you been going there, actually? And why haven't you told me?" I scream out in frustration. A long and deep cry from the center of my stomach to my bile-laced throat. I scream a scream to the golden sky in heartbreak and desperation. My energy quickens and rises, and I know I'll burst into flames if I don't release it soon!

"Blodwyn! Please!" she begs and throws herself at my feet.

"Sarah? Why did he call you *Sarah*, Sorcia? Have you betrayed me? Have you betrayed us?"

She weeps. Deep bellows from the pit of her soul emit from her lungs and out her mouth. Her woe, and sorrow, and shame sound like babies crying on a pyre as the tongues of the flames lick their flesh. "No! I swear. It was some ritual. He called it a baptism. It didn't mean anything. He put oil on my head and told me to pick a new name for their circle."

"Did he do this to Trond?" I scream.

"No! No! I wouldn't consent to it."

"Are you lying to me? Trond! Did you partake in any of these rituals? Speak now! Speak true!"

The frightened little boy furiously shakes his head, and I realize his fear is directed at me.

Peace, dear Brother. It's not you I am angry with. You have done no wrong. I say directly to his and Arik's minds. Arik places a reassuring hand on Trond's shoulder to calm him down.

I turn my attention back to the traitor at my feet. "Why would you do that? Why would you commit yourself to his false gods? And you spoke? About me? To him! What right does my name have coming from your lips? What makes you think it was sanctioned or even appropriate to reveal anything about us to strangers? Do you understand the danger you put yourself in? Us? Trond? Were you not thinking, Sorcia? Did you have some lapse of judgment or some out-of-body experience? Are you under the control of a draugr?"

My assault wounds her deeply, and she claws at my boots, desperate for me to understand words that have not yet left her brain. "Please, just hear me! He told us stories. Stories of a man... a man called Jesus," she stammers between sobs. Jesus was a great man! A wonderful and kind teacher. And he could do the most wonderous things."

I pause, my interest piqued. "And?"

"Michael said he had many followers and was crucified on a cross because of the things he said and did."

"Like what?" I inquire.

Sensing my willingness to listen to her, she quickly rises from the ground and pats the dirt from her pants. "Michael said Jesus could turn water into wine."

My face screws up with confusion. "He was killed for *that?* I could do that since I was Trond's age!"

"Michael said Jesus could walk on water."

"Not very impressive, Sorcia. Aizel can do that in her sleep."

"Michael said Jesus made a blind man see!"

Arik and I give each other a sly glance. We can't help but giggle. "Your point? I'm still not seeing the relevance or the greatness surrounding this man."

The anguish elevates in her voice as she realizes I am not at all impressed with the tales of this Jesus character. "He said he raised the dead! Michael said Jesus raised the dead!"

The world around me comes to a full stop and a deafening silence fills my head. All I hear are her words—the last sentence she spoke. The woodland creatures, and the setting sun, and the paper-thin cry of the locusts, all gasp and hold their breath.

She's certainly got my attention now.

"Jesus had a friend who died," she continues. She speaks rapidly so as to get every breathless word out. "Lazarus. His death upset Jesus so much that he went to Lazarus's tomb and raised him up from the dead."

"How? What else did he say? Did Michael explain how this Jesus person did it?"

"No, no. Nothing like that. But he's willing to talk, Blodwyn. And that's a start, right? I had to get involved with the group somehow. Anything to help you. Besides, Michael has many stories to share, I'm sure this is what we've been waiting for."

"Stories," I huff. "Don't confuse stories for proselytism. Michael and his people have only one goal in mind. No matter what they tell you, they want you to abandon your true nature and join their cause. And from the looks of things, you're pretty much already there... *Sarah*!"

"But that's my point, Blodwyn. I think this Jesus man was more like *us* than *they* realize. Michael calls him 'The Word made flesh.' Isn't that what Aizel called you because of your marks? The Word? *On your flesh?* That must be more than a coincidence. They also call Jesus the Shepherd. The *Shepherd*, Blodwyn! Modir spoke of a shepherd in her teachings. And all the miracles he performed! Miracles?" she laughs wildly. "Spells, Blodwyn! He worked spells! Things we were born just knowing how to do. Well, what if he was just like us? What if he had the blood of the old ones in his veins? What if the people who killed him knew this and tried to open the pathway for the ancients? Or to stop the ancients?"

I hate to admit it, but what Sorcia says rings true and clear within me. And with Arik, too. Her words painted pictures in my mind of a faraway land of sand and sun with white-robed men traversing the tundra and gathered around a gentle being they called Jesus—Yeshua, Brother, Teacher, Lord, The Redeemer, Savior, The Shepherd. Music swells in my head from the trees beyond the lakeside. Voices chant, and the drums play, and I swoon to the sound as it pulses in time with my heart and the burning of the runes against my flesh.

"Lazarus," I whisper. I hadn't wished to say the name out loud, but somehow it escaped me. "Lazarus," I say again, clearer, bolder.

Sorcia nods. "Raised from the dead."

"And Michael's sure about this?"

"I don't see why he would lie. It's part of his faith. Part of his religion."

"His religion…" I echo. "I think I've changed my mind, Sorcia. Go back to Michael and tell him I've reconsidered. Tell him I would be honored for him to pay a visit to our home. I'm very interested in the *stories* he's willing to share."

Chapter Eleven

In the Time of Darkness
In the Age of Ice
Summertime, 673 AD
Caverns in the Far North
Afternoon of the Full Moon

The tension in the cave wraps its hands around my throat and gently squeezes. I find it hard to squeak my words out every time Michael asks me a question, or when I'm obligated to ask one. It makes me warm. Warmer than I'm used to. Warmer than I'd like to be. Between the low burning fire in the center of the cave and the glowing tattoos on my flesh, I feel as if I could breathe actual fire. I've removed my cape and undershirt. My pinafore dress is secured with silver clasps, but it must look odd to the others with the bare skin of my branded arms in full view. If it makes them uncomfortable, I don't care. As a matter of fact, I want the outlander to be thrown off balance. And I want Sorcia to feel a sense of discomfort. I want her to understand the full magnitude of her actions. So be it—if she has brought us to this uncomfortable state, then why would she be free from the feeling?

Sorcia has arranged it so that Michael is to stay with us for three nights. It's part of his mission duties or something like that—the foundation of the work he was sent to do in our land. Part of this diplomatic exchange is for him to learn from us and, ultimately, teach us the principles of his faith with the hopes of gaining four more converts. Sorcia convinced him that, after much debate and lively conversation, I was interested in the work his group was doing and was interested in investigating things further. Of course, I was not, and Sorcia was fully aware of my true intentions. I agreed to the arrangement only for one reason—*learn more about the one called Lazarus.*

Aside from the introductory pleasantries and mindless small talk of "how was your journey here?" and "how long have you lived in town?" and "what is your native home like?" and "how long did it take you to learn our language?" it is very clear that Michael is an unwelcome outsider within our group. An outsider with dark hair and dark eyes and the grin of a snake meant to do us harm. Only he knows not the true nature of snakes. That much I gleaned right away. Sorcia's overly friendly gestures and the higher octave of her usual speaking voice indicate her desperation to have this meeting go well. She wants me to like him. She wants me to approve of him in some twisted way. And while she has assured me that she has arranged this gathering for my benefit, I can't help but think she's done it more for herself than anyone else. A stroke of her hand playfully down his arm, and a loud, obnoxious giggle are more telling than the words that come from her lips. She delights in him. Cares for him. Even if she hasn't admitted it to herself yet, there's something there. Something deeper. Michael is an outsider, much like herself, and I suspect she finds that comforting.

Regardless, we sit and chat and take turns asking our questions of each other, yet Arik sits silently at my side. He's poised at the ready for an attack against me. His energy seethes off him in purple waves. I rub his knee affectionately to let him know I am aware of his protective stance, and he smiles at my touch. Michael notices the gesture and remarks. "Blodwyn, you are not yet married? Aren't women in your culture married much younger?"

Aizel coughs as if something was stuck in her throat, and I feel Arik's body stiffen.

"Aye," I say. "Our circumstances are a bit different. My mother passed giving birth to Trond, and I took on full responsibility for him. Thankfully, I've had Aizel and Sorcia to help me raise him. So no, I have not had that luxury."

"But you two," he turns to look at Sorcia and Aizel, "why have you not sought a hand?"

Sorcia opens her mouth to answer, but I jump in. "Loyalty. They are loyal to me, to my mother, to the oaths they took years ago. When you commit to something, it is honorable to see it through. You of all people should know that."

Michael sighs. A knowing sigh. "Quite right. But Arik? How does he fit into your equation?"

I don't like his tone with that question. It seems as if he's trying to accuse me of something—accuse *us* of something. I look around the fire. "You see us," I say. "Three women and a young child. Quite the vulnerable lot, wouldn't you say? Arik protects us. Watches over us. We're a family."

Michael raises an eyebrow into a perfect black, bushy arch that seems to reach the top of his hairline.

Sorcia shifts her body closer to him, one of her legs slips inconspicuously into his lap. "Arik takes care of us, and we take care of his sick wife," she says, and that desperation in her voice again makes my ears bleed.

Michael's tongue clicks against the roof of his mouth with a 'tsk' sound. "Oh!" he gushes, "I've heard that you are capable of taking care of yourselves."

Arik shifts his legs, and I squeeze the top of his knee to settle him down.

Words, I say into his mind. *Just words.*

Aizel rises from the circle, and Trond gets up to follow her. They return to us, and Trond passes us each a cup. Aizel walks daintily around us, pouring the liquid into each of our glasses and humming a happy tune. She smiles slyly at me as Sorcia's irritation mounts.

Chapter Eleven

"Remember when we first met, Michael, I said your wine tasted like death?"

He holds his cup steady as Aizel pours water into it. The clear liquid brims the top rim of the chalice. "Thank you," he says to her, then turns his attention back to me. "Yes, yes, Blodwyn. I remember."

Aizel pours mine. I thank her in our ancient tongue and Michael's head cocks to the side with curiosity. "Well, now you'll get a taste of what real fruit wine tastes like."

He laughs. A closed mouth, inside chuckle that makes my skin burn. "What are you talking about? This is water in my cup."

"Is it?" I ask, and with a flick of my hand, I send a wave of energy across the room directed at his chest. He jolts from my sting. His face drops with sudden fear and uncertainty. It's Trond now who lets out a stifled giggle.

"Can I have some too, Blodwyn?" he whines.

"Later, Trond," I say forcefully, keeping my glare on Michael.

"Blodwyn! Stop!" Sorcia admonishes.

But I ignore her. "Drink," I command him. "Tell me that it's not the best fruit wine you've ever had."

Michael looks at Sorcia eagerly, like a child looking for acknowledgement. His pale face drained of color and replaced with fear. It's the same, pathetic face she'd given me, and again, their connection to me is clear. *They are of the same ilk.* Sorcia nods as if to tell him it's alright to drink, and he does. The pink hue returns to his cheeks when the wine fills his mouth. He gulps it down with harsh gurgles in his throat like he can't get enough. Like he's never had anything so sweet and satisfying before.

He exhales with an "Ahhh" and looks about the room—a sudden expression of doubt and shame invades his eyes. "But it was..." he stammers.

I stand up, walk over to him, and reach out my hand. "You have stories, so I've heard. And you're open to having a dialogue, so I've heard. Let's make that happen, shall we?" Hesitantly, he puts his hand in mine, and I help yank him up from the rocky floor. "Michael and I are going to have a conversation," I announce to the group. Sorcia's eyes go wide. They are round and black with terror and anxiety. Blue runes flicker above her head as she worries about what I might say to Michael when I'm alone with him. He recognizes her uneasiness as well and gives her a nod to reassure her everything is fine. She exhales, and her shoulders slightly relax. But she's rattled. And I don't care.

"Come, my friend. Walk with me," I say and lead him through the orange glow of the cavern hallway.

Michael follows in step with me as I bring him to my private chambers at the far end of the cave. We pass by Ylfa's alcove, and her gurgling makes him stop in his tracks. He gasps when the full sight of her sitting in her chair comes into view behind the dancing shadows of the hallway torches. He tugs at my wrist, forcing me to stop and look as well. Michael's interest in her emaciated frame sparks my own, and I fully take in the pathetic vision. It has been so long since I looked at Ylfa—I mean, really looked at her. For seven years, she was just *there*. But at this moment, I look at her how Michael must see her—a frail, haggard mute of a woman (or what once resembled a woman) slumped over in her chair with her long, matted hair sweeping the rock floor. Her shoulders rock from side to side like she is in a permanent state of convulsion, and her hollow eyes stare off into the distance to the beyond, through the beyond. They are so sunken in that in the wavey light of the lanterns they look like two gaping holes gouged in her gray-skin face. Black voids of nothingness.

Until Modir comes back and fills her shell back with life.

She starts to hum—a low dirge rattling in the center of her chest. Its sound is discordant and off-tune. There is no rhyme or reason in the melody, and the timbre of it startles Michael to his core.

Poor Ylfa. I wonder where she is right now.

"That's Arik's wife," I say and nudge his shoulder.

"W… what's wrong with her?" he stammers. Shock and disgust drip from his voice.

"Sorcia told you she was unwell. We help take care of her," I say matter-of-factly.

"But she… she… she's not…"

"Not well," I reiterate. "This way," I say and urge him to follow me further through the cave.

He shuts his mouth with a quick popping sound and doesn't say another word until we reach my room. I bustle in, light the torches at each corner, and bid him to enter. With much hesitation, he crosses the threshold and looks around the room. Quickly, he notices Arik's clothing bunched up at the foot of the bed and points at the pile. "But you're not married!" he admonishes. "He has a wife to whom he made a promise to, did he not?"

Instinctively, a hand goes to my hip, and I shift my weight from side to side. "Oh, dear Michael!" I sing. "You speak our language very well, which is honorable, for our common tongue is not easy to learn. We are harsh and sharp of sound, and you seem to have immersed yourself quite nicely. Yet, no matter how fluent you are, your accent gives you away. It was one of the first things I noticed when I met you. It reveals you, shows your true nature. You speak our language, but not everything translates so literally. There are phrases that have different nuances. An exaggerated syllable here, or a pressed sound there—a multitude of permutations that your foreigner's ear could never learn or understand. These little things will always mark you as an outsider."

Michael sighs and crosses his arms behind him as if he's steeling himself to the granite floor. "Your people certainly are complex, aren't they?" He gives a little nervous laugh.

Chapter Eleven

I smile back at him, but there is no joy behind it. It is a smile of domination. A smile of knowing. A smile that lets him know I am, and always will be, in control. "Yes. But they are not my people. Not really. Yes, I am from them—their blood, their lines, their culture. But I am not truly part of them. I walk among them, but I am not one of them."

"Oh, so you're an outsider too?" he mocks.

The tattoos on my arms flash red with a surge of anger. Michael takes a step back in fear, and the color drains from his face again. He narrows his eyes as his mind desperately tries to rationalize what it is he saw. I can see the questions forming at the precipice of his mind—the deep canyon that separates a man from madness and reality: *Was that a reflection from the torch? Is my mind playing tricks on me? How did she do that?*

His brain tells his mouth to say, "How did you do that?" to which I give a soft chuckle.

"Would you like to see it again?" I tease, and the energy inside me crescendos to a burning climax so that every rune emblazoned on my flesh turns red again. Like a blazing fire, I light up the room, drowning out the glow from the torches. I throw my head back so that the markings on my neck are also in full sight—so he can marvel in my supreme glory. The hair on my arms sizzles and singes as the scent of burnt hair and flesh fills the room.

Michael closes his eyes to shut out the miracle before him. "Our Father who art in heaven..." he mumbles.

Immediately, I shut the energy down, stopping the heat flow and returning to my normal, pale hue. "Allfather?" I ask.

"What was that? What are you?" His voice is shaky. Scared.

"You pray to Odin, Michael? The Allfather." I say, ignoring his questions.

He stiffens, as if I've dishonored him, and musters up courage from somewhere deep inside. He swallows hard. "Our. I said, 'our Father.' It's the Lord's prayer. One of the many teachings of Christ."

"All. Our. Isn't it the same, really?"

"Do *you* worship the one they call Odin, Blodwyn?"

"Oh, no. No. Odin. Thor. Freya," I say as I saunter to my bed. "They are but names and imagined bodies with personalities. Something tangible the people created to make the old ones real. But the ancients have no names, not ones that most humans could comprehend anyway. And their faces? Most people would freeze in their tracks and die a sudden death should they look upon their splendor, for human eyes can't see beyond what's in front of them. They can't look into the sky and visualize just how vast this world is, let alone conceptualize the span of what is elsewhere. But I know, Michael. I know the beauty the old ones possess. And one day, they will grace this world again and reclaim what is rightfully theirs." I pat the empty space next to me, bidding him to join. He does, but there is caution and hesitation in his movements. "That's better. If we're to share the tenets of our faiths with each other, we might as well do it in comfort."

He shifts a little—clearly, he is *un*comfortable—and he clears his throat.

"Why did your people come to our land?" I ask. "And don't tell me that it was a deal brokered by your chieftain and mine or that it was for the greater good or any of that. Why did you, Michael from the Otherlands, come here, to the Frostheim? Personally. What was your true motivation?"

But he stares at me in disbelief and ignores my inquiry. "Your arms," he says, pointing at me. "Your chest. Your neck. Those aren't just tattoos, are they?"

"Oh, Michael," I sigh, "I don't think this is how dialogue works. You see, you can't answer a question with a question—especially an unrelated question. If we're going to be open and honest with each other and come to an understanding, then we're going to have to..."

"I've seen the people in the village with their warrior brands, but yours are different. Yours are... are... *alive.*" He whispers the last word as if he's in a state of disbelief.

"I am the Story. The History. The runes imprinted themselves on my body to carry on the legacy of the Blodheksa. I am the word made flesh," I say, and with a flick of my index finger, a glittery wave of light surrounds us for a moment.

His eyes twinkle at my magic—mesmerized by the power before him. Quickly, he blinks as if to erase what he saw and come back to his safe reality. "Impossible!" he exclaims indignantly. "There was only one man. One man who was the Word made flesh—the Word of God—who fulfilled all the biblical prophecies. Jesus Christ."

I don't want to push him too hard or too far, for I feel his dedication to his beliefs is so strong that if I say the wrong thing, I won't be able to get the answers I need. For there is much I can learn from him—I just know it. I need to be a little gentler and more understanding. "And just who is this man?" I say, toning down my voice. "And why do you believe so deeply in him? You've gone so far as to seduce one of my oldest and dearest friends to the point where I question her loyalty. So, tell me. Tell me the stories of the one *you* serve."

"God, the Father, who art in heaven, sent his only son, Jesus, to be born among the humans. He was a wonderful man. A great teacher and leader who had many disciples and followers. People who believed in him. People who gave up everything they had just to be in his presence. He helped the poor, cured the sick, raised the dead—many miracles he performed to show the world he was the one true Son of God. He eventually was crucified by the empire because he scared them all. His power was too great, and the government saw him as a threat to their hierarchy. But when he died, we believe he saved us all. His sacrifice opened the gates of heaven and all the souls of the faithfully departed rose to meet God and to love in eternal paradise. Jesus was crucified. Died. And was buried. And on the third day, he rose from the dead—free from the shackles of death and appeared to his most devout disciples one last time. Then on the highest hill, Jesus transfigured—a blinding light shone from within and around him and he was lifted to eternal rest to be with his Father, the Lord our God, forever." He pauses and takes in a deep breath. "Of course, there's more. There's so much more," he exhales wildly. "That is merely the abbreviated version."

My level of curiosity has certainly been elevated, and I begin to understand the appeal the story may have had on Sorcia. I, too, am intrigued. I, too, am secretly interested to hear more of this mysterious Jesus.

He reminds me of me.

"And when Sorcia comes to your meetings, you tell her these stories?"

"The in-depth versions, yes. My group reads from our Bible. Sarah has been learning our tongue."

My head cocks to the side sharply. "Oh," escapes my lips.

"She never told you?"

I shake my head. "Where did Jesus get his power from? Sorcia told me he raised his friend Lazarus from the dead. Now you're saying he also raised *himself* from the dead? How is that possible? You say he performed spells..."

"Miracles," he corrects.

"Words," I answer curtly. "Were they tricks? Or did he really do the things you said? How can you be sure? You speak of stories passed down over ages hence, how do you know it isn't lies and speculation? How do you know he wasn't just an illusionist?"

"Faith, Blodwyn. We believe because we have faith in God the Father, and God the Son, and God the Holy Spirit."

"There's a draugr involved, too?"

His face screws up with confusion. "A what?"

I wave my hand in the air. "Nothing, nothing."

"How do you know what you say is true, Blodwyn? Aren't your beliefs based on stories from ages hence?"

A smile spreads across my face, and I raise my arms in the air above my head twisting them from side to side. "You see this, right? This is *my* Bible. I believe because I've seen things. I believe because I can do things. Now, let me tell you a story. And at the end, I think you'll agree—we might be more closely aligned than you think."

I flick my index finger again in the air and create a thick, glowing atmosphere around us. Startled, Michael grips the side of my wooden bed. The skin of his knuckles flushes white with fear as a red haze fills the sacred space. A drumming sound starts out low in the distance. It grows louder and louder and is layered with a rising song. *The* song. The song of the old ones beckoning me home. Their voices are shrill and crackly and filled with their ancient magics, and the swoon of their cacophony makes my tattoos shimmer in wavey light.

I'm not going to tell you, I say directly into his mind. *I'm going to show you. Be not afraid, Michael. I go before you, always.*

Chapter Twelve

Before Time Was
At the Breath of Creation
In the Chaos of the Universe

In the beginning, there was a void. A great chasm that stretched from one end of the cosmos to the next. An enormous, all engulfing and all-consuming space of emptiness. Of nothingness. Of everything and nothing, and everywhere and nowhere all at once. Slowly, very slowly, the void began to spit out shapes from deep within its bowels like it was vomiting the chaos from its system. Circular masses of all colors and sizes spewed forth with violent atmospheres of fire and ice. They hovered and maneuvered themselves throughout the void, which eventually turned out to not be much of a gaping expanse of desolation anymore. In fact, the universe was teeming with objects that screamed, and burned, and stormed, and *lived*. The universe was now filled with the chasm's belly by-products and was transformed into a glowing, lively

entity that sparkled with a variety of colors and brilliance.

The atmosphere within the very first celestial bodies was violent and not conducive to harboring life. The early fires and storms and gasses combined to shape each planet individually, leaving some completely barren while others were left rife with multicell organisms. But at the first dawning of this world, a light from the cosmos charged down from what was left of the chasm—the last remnants of bile from its belly—and pierced the sky with a blinding flash and a screeching howl. The light burrowed itself deep in a mountainside of fire where it festered and grew and took shape—many shapes. Soon, many shapes and figures emerged from where the light had opened the land. Many shapes and figures reached their many arms and legs and heads and faces through the wreckage of the scar. The old ones. The ancients. The first beings to step foot on the solid ground of this world.

Their beautiful and twisted bodies danced wildly under the red haze of the fire sky. Their movements created the clouds and set the poison waters to learn the dance of the tides. When they sang their dirges in their low bellow-y voices, the song resonated across the entire world and cemented land to earth and shook the grass up from its slumber.

And they reigned. And ruled. And lived freely by their own will and design. From the largest of them—the size of gargantuan monoliths—to the smallest of them—as small as fawns—they lived and bred, and by the power of their instincts and ancient magic, they fashioned the world as they saw fit. They created language and thought, feeling and emotion, and pleasure and pain (with no real distinction between the two). They ate what they wanted, killed what they wanted, loved what they wanted, created what they wanted, and coupled with whomever they wanted. When violence overcame them and fighting broke out, the skies rained down with their blood and seeped into the very pores of the soil. From their blood mixed with the earth rose all kinds of plant life and vegetation as the world they inhabited continued to grow and shift and change. And because of the old ones' eternal lifespan, they chose if and when they wanted to retire back into the breath of the cosmos

And it was good.

When the mood struck them right, they mated all at once in a passionate frenzy—a celebration of wanton lust and desire. With their spilled seed, that too created all different forms of life from insects to water creatures. As time passed, the ancient ones copulated thousands of times over, bringing forth generation after generation of hideous and beautiful beings. But from a well-spring in one of the more verdant lands, a new life form had multiplied undetected, and their existence perplexed the ancients. This was man and woman—the first of their kind, an evolutionary culmination of the old ones' design from a long-forgotten creation. Evolution went unchecked.

Until now.

Curious, the old ones captured some of the humans and held them for their own delights, interested in understanding the functions of their forms. The ones they confiscated were held in the forges and ravaged both day and night in the most brutal of ways. The offspring produced from the old ones and the mystery breed was not viable, often resulting in painful and savage deaths for both mother and child. And the same held true for the old ones—if the seed of a human male was made to penetrate one of the beings, the child would not survive the birth. Eventually, the old ones grew tired and weary of trying to mate with the humans, and once again ignored them, leaving them to their own devices. The humans settled on the outskirts of the world—mindful of the old ones and keeping their distance so as to live in peace.

But then something changed.

A child was born of woman and beast. A live birth. A female child with the shape of a human and the power and strength of the old ones. It was truly a sight to behold. All beings from all over the world came to rejoice in the miracle! A celebration was held as they dubbed the child *Blodheksa*— the Blood Witch who would rule them all.

But the ancients got greedy, and soon, some of them wanted their own Blodheksas—a strong woman who would represent their own bloodline as the supreme class. The raping of the humans began again as the race to produce such a being ensued. The unions ended mostly the same, with the same gnarled offspring with misshapen forms. Only a few true aberrations were born—female children born of woman and monster. The ten children born formed a schism amongst the deities, and much to the dismay of the ancients, ten clans banded together with the children as their boons of salvation: their familial Blodheksas. It was a dark time even for the foulest of the foul, for never had there been a division among them.

Soon, the Blodheksas, realizing their tremendous power, began squabbling among themselves over blood rights and positions and spellcraft—things that meant nothing to the ancients. Their human sides got the better of them, and they began to express their own intentions. Each one vastly different from the other, the Blodheksas couldn't agree upon what their exact role was in their homes, society, culture, and in the world.

One of man's greatest downfalls is his avarice and his quest for power. Unfortunately, the Blodheksas were not free from this propensity. One of the ten, Bkär the Traitor, lead the charge with the others against the old ones. She united them against their predecessors claiming the first beings were evil and needed to be eliminated. Hungry to be the only beings of magic in the world, Bkär planned to use the power of the Blodheksas to imprison and banish them. Because of their immortality, Bkär knew they would not

be able to destroy the ancients, so she and eight
of the ten used the magics of dark and light and
sex to create an elemental plane not of this world
to trap them in forever so they could have complete domination over the earth without living
in the literal shadows of behemoths. They toiled
tirelessly day and night to perfect their spell.

But Evanak disagreed with Bkär. She was the
only Blodheksa who was content with the shape
of the world and loved her kin, so she left the
group when she realized the eventual war was
coming. She hid among the other humans by the
well-spring and verdant plains, and when Bkär
launched the attack, Evanak kept her human
group well-protected from the onslaught.

The battle raged for what seemed like an eternity. The tumult of the magical dance cracked
mountains open and split landmasses in half.
The poison seas rose and washed away chunks
of earth, dragging them down to the depths of
the ocean floor. All was decimated and left in
ruin, and in the end, Bkär was successful in expel-
ling the beings to the other realm; however, she
and the eight other Blodheksas were killed in
the process.

When the smoke cleared and the dust settled and there was no more chaos and suffering
on land and sea, Evanak emerged from under-
ground with the group of one hundred people
she had protected. Those people set out into the
world to regroup, rebuild, and repopulate. By
her side stood Audrm, a human man she had

fallen in love with while in hiding. And in her arms two children nestled close to her chest—a boy and a girl—the Blodbrødre and Blodsøster. Evanak raised her head to the sky and shrieked. She promised that one day she would call the old ones back home. She promised she would free them from their celestial prison. She promised she would tear open the sky and sing out in victory as they tumbled through the realms and back to their rightful place on earth. Because if Bkär, the Traitor, could use the power from nine of the original Blodheksas to seal them away, then she would be the one last stronghold for their return. All was not lost. Evanak was determined to find a way.

In the Time of Darkness
In the Age of Ice
Summertime, 673 AD
Caverns in the Far North
Evening of the Full Moon

I wave my hand and the red haze dissipates in front of our eyes. Michael stands in the center of the room. His dark eyes blink rapidly, and it is obvious his brain is still trying to process the visuals I presented to him. He told me his story—I showed him mine. He still does not understand the full extent of my power. I am not surprised.

"I… I don't understand," he stammers softly.

Chapter Twelve

A brisk "tsk" of my tongue against the roof of my mouth fills the room. "I'm not sure how else to explain it to you. I thought I showed you a good amount of…"

"Showed me. How? How were you able to do that?" He's mystified, and the look in his eyes tells me he's still searching the deepest parts of his memory to recall my images. He's surveying the landscape of his brain so as to hold on to the red-hazed world I brought him to.

I shrug my shoulders. "How am I able to do anything I am capable of? I am from a long line of Blodheksas. From the blood of Evanak."

"I don't believe you," he says, his voice presenting with a touch of gravel in it like leather shoes scraping against stone. "That was just an illusion, a fantasy. I don't know what trickery you weave, but that wasn't real. There was no such being named Evanak. I have never read of it in my scriptures. There was Anak, in the Old Testament. He was the son of Arba and the father of a race of big men who ruled over the land of Canaan. You somehow got into my head, or knew my texts, but whatever it is, whatever you know, you create trickery."

"Trickery? I put before you the wonder of my power, and you call it trickery? Did you not walk through the veil of time with me? Did you not smell the acrid air of the red-hazed landscape? Did you not feel the ground shake when the giant monoliths glided across the world drumming their cloven hooves to the beat of their hearts?

Did you not hear the cries of the humans and the old ones? You reference a book you read. A book that was written long before your existence, and here I am—I take you through the vision quest of time and show you what truly happened, what transpired! Events that no man could translate or put into words, and you..."

"Enough!" he shouts and puts his hands up in surrender. "Enough. I need to think. I need to collect myself. I fear you poisoned me. Put something in my wine."

"Oh, you mean the water that Aizel poured that I *turned* to wine?"

He stares at me blankly.

"You didn't do that. You would be implying that..."

"I am like the one you serve. And what is so wrong with that? Only he could perform what you call miracles? Didn't you ever stop to think that maybe there were others like him? Others with abilities beyond compare."

He shakes his head maniacally. "No. No. Jesus is the son of God. Creator of heaven and earth. The Lord sent him to be the redeemer of man's sins."

"Words," I huff.

"Faith," he retorts. "Faith above all."

"And if not for faith, then what? You never saw this man, the one called Jesus. Never met him. Never bore witness to these miracles he presumably performed. Yet, you still believe. With your whole heart and *fylgja*, you believe that he existed, and you believe he was powerful. Blindly. And here I stand before you. You've drank the water I turned to wine. You've met the blind man I gave sight to. You see the markings on my body that brand me as the word. And you walked with me on the edge of time. What more will it take for you to believe what your own eyes have shown you? Jesus is your god of countless stories. But me? I am nothing but lies and deception? Seems like you're the one who's truly blind. Or is the story I shared too close to home for you? Is it too real that your mind refuses to admit its validity?"

"To admit your truth would mean to abandon mine."

"Not abandon, Michael. Truth is a transformative concept. There is nothing wrong with admitting you were wrong. In fact, it's quite the opposite. It's a noble and honorable trait."

"I cannot. I cannot accept your words as truth."

"To deny your eyes is to deny your god."

"My God knows what's in my heart, Blodwyn. Does yours?"

"God doesn't exist, Michael. At least not in the sense that you've been trained to believe. The power, the energy, the primordial forces that violently forged their way into existence are all there is. Your Jesus is a part of that lifeforce. That lifeforce will come again, and I will be its harbinger."

"So, according to what you've told me, you're saying you are a Blodheksa?"

I take a step back in defense. "Oh no! No, no, no! My role has changed many times and I'm still trying to figure that out. My mother holds that title. She is the true Blodheksa. Modir. She will be the one to rip open the sky and set the old ones free from their prison."

He grows silent. Pensive. I know my words and actions have done nothing to convince him. His faith is steadfast—bolted into the icy earth and rooted deep within the hollows of the planet. It's unwavering. Unmovable. "Tell me, Michael," I say after a moment of silence, "what did you hope to gain by coming here and meeting with me?"

"You tell me—what did you hope to gain by inviting me into your home?"

"Discourse. Knowledge. An exchange of ideas. A chance to show you that your savior and I are very much alike. Kin, possibly. And you? What were your intentions?"

"Let's not pretend, Blodwyn. You know exactly what my intentions are. You know exactly what my sole mission is."

"Conversion," I say bluntly.

"And that's not happening, is it?"

"Not today, Michael. Not today. Nor do I presume there would be a conversion on your part?"

"No, Blodwyn. My Bible teaches that the Devil is all-knowing, and he is crafty enough to show us evil in the form of many beautiful things." He smiles brightly at me, like he thinks he's won. "Sarah knows that. She realizes that what you have here is evil. I helped her see the way. She will leave you, Blodwyn. She will come and join me and spread the true word of God."

Chapter Twelve

His words sting me like the way the flesh on your knees shreds up after falling and sliding on jagged gravel. This time, I don't believe him, but I can't help but stop and wonder if I'm just trying to convince myself. Doubt flashes in my eyes, and a little grin upturns on the side of his mouth. Refusing to give him the upper hand, I smile back coyly. "There is no devil, Michael. No good or evil. Just the scales. The balance. Maybe one day you'll see that. And as for Sorcia," I pause, emphasizing her real name and not the made-up bastardized one he's given her, "she's not going anywhere. Remember, I told you about loyalty. She will remain with me forever and beyond if I ask her to. Our bond isn't so easily broken. It is the way of our people."

He pauses, absorbing my words, but makes no direct response. "We should return to the others," he finally says.

"One last thing, though. Lazarus. The one your savior raised from the dead. How did he do it?"

"There was no formula or ritual or secret words or incantations if that's what you mean."

"Then how?"

"It's very simple, Blodwyn. Jesus wept."

Chapter Thirteen

In the Time of Darkness
In the Age of Ice
Summertime, 673 AD
Caverns in the Far North
Early Morning of the Waning Gibbous Moon

Two moontides passed, and for all his denials and adamant refusals to believe what is right in front of him, Michael decided to stay. I thought for sure after my vision quest with him, he would have left immediately to go back to his village, but I was wrong. He stayed, claiming he still had more to learn and understand, but Aizel was suspicious of his motives. She told me she believes that his intentions are to report us to the Jarl. Rumor has it that the Jarl is very close to aligning himself with the missionaries, and Aizel is afraid we will be the first social sacrifice of the old ways. For when they kill Odin and Thor, we are not too far behind.

But I didn't mind; I allowed Michael to remain with us for as long as he liked. I had nothing to hide. I didn't mind his suspicious eyes wandering about—let him look, let him learn. Maybe what he sees will awaken something in him. I doubt it. Tell the Jarl, don't tell the Jarl. It matters not, for I know there is nothing they could possibly do to us that would bring us harm. Our power runs deep and wide, and I have scores of protection spells at my fingertips. Besides, I was still pondering the things he said—things about Sorcia and things about his Jesus.

Day breaks, and I sit up in my bed with swarming thoughts humming in my mind like bees dancing all around me. Musical notes of murmurs lilt throughout the cave, and I soon realize people are talking in hushed voices so as to not wake the others. But I can hear them perfectly well if I concentrate hard enough. I shuffle off the side of the bed frame and wrap my bear skin blanket across my shoulders. Even the summers bring cool air deep into the cave, and I like the way the bristly fur feels coarse at the surface and soft and billowy underneath. I don't need to wrap myself in it, really. But I enjoy petting it when it's on me.

Silently, I tip-toe to the front of the cave and hide behind one of the rock pillars. Trond and Aizel are mulling about the altar, and his little voice is chattering wildly. She's a good teacher for him. A good guide. Sometimes I think she's better than I am with him. When he was five, I had tried to teach him how to expel his first draugr from a boy his own age. It didn't go as planned, to say the least. I guess I had underestimated Trond's natural abilities and the magnitude of his power, and the little boy with the demon inside him ended up dying in the process. I was stupid and eager and hadn't considered the power of the Blodbrødre would have had such an effect. And Trond was too young. It was my fault for being so enthusiastic to begin teaching him with such an intense ritual.

When Trond was three, he called me "Modir," and I didn't react very well to that. I smacked him across the face and yelled at him for saying such a thing. "Modir is gone, Ruz!" I screamed at him. "Modir was taken away! But I will fix that. Mark my words. I swear it by the sky, and the moon, and the sun, and the stars, and the fixed iced earth, and the great beyond! I will slice open the sky and pull her back through the circle. For she is the Blodheksa, the Blood Witch who will open the gateway. And I am the Blodsøster, the Blood Sister who will aid the Blodheksa in her mission." I pointed my forefinger and jabbed it deep into the crook of his shoulder. "And you are the Blodbrødre, the Blood Brother who will fight by my side for eternity in the new world. This is how it must be."

He ran off to his chambers in hysterics, and I just stood there, cold, and unfeeling. It wasn't until Aizel came over and talked me down from my anger. She said I needed to have more patience with him—that he didn't really know what a mother was and that I was the closest thing to being one for him. "He's still so young," she said. "He doesn't fully understand the words you speak." I took in what she said—took it straight into my heart—and realized I was wrong for being so cross with him. If not for Aizel, I probably would have still carried that anger toward him to this very day. She is gentle in a way that I can't afford to be. I need to be abrasive and direct, but it is sometimes at the cost of hurting the ones I love so very much.

Trond.

My sweet Ruz.

I would do anything for him. Anything. He is the only other being in the world who shares Modir's blood with me. We are of the same essence—the male and female construct from Modir. We are the Blodsøster and the Blodbrødre. The fierce, protective love I have for him is very much like what a mother would have for a child. But I want his real mother to be here for him. I want him to know her and be taught by her. I feel it in my bones, it will happen soon.

"She was beautiful," Aizel says, and I tune in my senses to their conversation. "Her hair was so long and red. Not orange like some of the women in the village. It was dark red, like blood."

Ah. She's regaling him with stories of Modir.

"Like yours?" Trond asks, his sweet little voice lilting upward in wonder of Aizel's tale.

"Darker!" she muses. "Sometimes if the sun's rays caught the color just right, it would look almost purple."

"Wow! That's unbelievable."

169

"She was a pretty unbelievable woman," she answers matter-of-factly. "She taught me everything I know, but most of all she trusted me and let me become who I needed to become. She trusted in the power inside me and let me figure out how to use it properly. She was a wonderful teacher and a wonderful guide because she believed in me."

My body tenses up, and I realize Aizel knows I'm there, lurking in the background. I was born, but I wasn't born yesterday! I know her little wisdom trinket is more for me than it is for Trond.

Point taken, I say directly into her mind, and she lets out a soft giggle in response.

"You know, Trond, your mother always believed in you too. She was adamant that you were alive in her belly all those years. When everyone called her crazy and didn't believe her, she held onto the truth of your existence."

"Do you think Blodwyn believes in me?" he asks innocently.

My body tenses up again as I anticipate her response. My heart breaks a little to think that he would even question my love or faith in him.

"Why ever would you ask me that?" she gushes. "Of course she does! You know everything Blodwyn does is with you in mind. You know how important you are! Don't ever think otherwise."

He lowers his head as if he has more to say as if there's more in his heart and in his mind, but he is bound to the capacity of his human seven-year-old self. He shuffles one foot in front of the other, scraping the soles of his leather boots against the rocky floor.

"No, no," Aizel admonishes. "You're wrong. Blodwyn has a lot of responsibilities and has much work to do. She's been working so hard. She's been trying for many years now."

Aizel addresses him as if he'd spoken, but I'm standing right here, and I know my ears heard not his voice. Suddenly, it dawns on me that not only has he spoken to her telepathically, but both were able to close themselves off to any outsider trying to tap into their private conversation. I have been completely shut off from them. A wave of uneasiness bubbles up from the pit of my stomach and my tattoos throb with an orange light in sync with my heartbeat.

"You know how powerful she is, Trond," Aizel continues. "Everything comes so easily to her, except this one thing. She must be so frustrated that she hasn't been able to bring Modir back."

"I want to help her," he says eagerly.

She giggles again and rubs the top of his blond hair. "Trust me! You will. When she is ready, you will be the first by her side."

He smiles brightly at her.

"You're important to her." She bends down and whispers in his ear. "You're more important than Sorcia, that's for sure. You're even more important than me!"

His gray eyes go wide with pride and wonder. "You think so?"

"I know so," she reassures.

"When Blodwyn brings Modir back, what will she be like? What will she look like?"

"I don't know for sure. None of us have ever done that before, nor have we ever witnessed it."

He crinkles his nose. "I think she'll be scary. Just bones walking around."

Aizel pulls him into her and presses his face to the side of her thigh. "Oh no! Sweet boy! Don't think like that! Please. Don't be afraid of what she'll look like. That's one of the things that Blodwyn is working on. I know she won't bring Modir back in a way to frighten you. No, no! That's why we have Ylfa too. Everyone has a part to play."

"Modir will look like Ylfa?"

"If Blodwyn does it right, then yes."

"Will Modir *be* Ylfa?" he asks, the curiosity dripping from his tongue.

"No. Her *fylgja* would be in Ylfa's body. Ylfa's *fylgja* would go into the ground with Modir's body."

"Oh," he says softly. "Ylfa loves me. She took care of me."

Aizel releases him and kneels beside him so that her face meets his. "Oh," she asks quizzically. "How do you know that?"

"I remember. I remember everything."

"You do? How much?"

He shrugs his shoulders. "I dunno. All of it."

"Do you remember being born?"

"Yeah," he answers nonchalantly. "And before that, too."

"Wow!" she crows, but there's a hint of concern in her voice that she tries hard to hide from him.

From me.

Before I have a chance to think on it further, a searing pain needles its way at the base of my skull and up to the center of my head. I hear chimes in the distance, and a feeling of intense pressure builds up behind my eyes. There's only one thing that can make me feel that way — Arik calling for me with urgency. I want so badly to stay and listen to the rest of their conversation and decode the nuances that pass silently between them, but in the pit of my stomach, Arik's call to me is far more pressing. I will have to deal with Trond later.

Without further hesitation, I shift my mind's eye over to align with Arik and tune into what he so desperately needed my attention on. The vision presented before me freezes me in place. Horrified, I have no idea how Arik bears witness to the scene, and truthfully, I'd rather not know, but there in Sorcia's room I see her and Michael in a compromising position. The two naked bodies kneel facing each other on her bed. Michael's manhood is thin and long like a small sword. It looks like it's dancing in the open space between him and the upper part of her stomach.

And his hands with the long, thin fingers that look like mini versions of his organ grab her breasts and bring them to his mouth. He takes a peach-colored nipple and nibbles at it gently between his teeth before clamping his whole mouth down to suckle on her. She throws her head back and squeals with pleasure as she reaches her hand down between his legs, grabs his shaft, and runs her hands up and down with feverish motions. It unnerves me to watch them touch each other like that. Something about it doesn't feel right.

Where are you, Arik? I say to him. *How are you able to...*

But he shuts his eyes tightly causing the vision stream to go dark. That's my cue to stop talking and just observe. *Fine!* I relent, and he opens his eyes again.

Michael kisses her hard, then leans over and whispers in her ear. She smiles and giggles, and her pale face flushes with hot pink. The color of her cheeks are like a flower garden in full bloom. "No! No! You can't!" she squeals again with laughter. He whispers again, and she laughs a little softer. "Well, that I can do," she says coyly and bends her upper body onto him, taking his manhood in her mouth. He clutches the back of her head and thrust his hips wildly into her mouth that for a second I fear she's going to choke on his narrow shaft. Like it might go directly down her mouth and get lodged in her throat!

"Oh, God," he moans. "How I wish this wasn't your mouth. Please, Sarah, I want to be one with you!"

Chapter Thirteen

I suspect she told him she still had her maidenhead. If he still believed that after the way she worked him with her mouth, he was denser than I originally thought.

Arik chuckles at my thought, and I send him a *shhh*.

We all knew Sorcia was knowledgeable in the ways of sex. Probably more than any of us combined. And I knew she wouldn't be able to keep up the charade of her virginity for much longer because her blood ran hot, and her sex throbbed purple, and if there was one thing Sorcia loved above all, it was love—passion and the intensity of the act of desire. It fueled her. Drove her.

She stops her head-bobbing motions, pulls away from his grasp, turns her back to him, and gets on all fours on the bed. "Are... are you sure? I don't want this to be... I ... I don't want to hurt you or..." he stammers in disbelief.

Without saying a word, she spreads her legs open for him. The scent of her sweet honey wafts in the room. The very smell of her drives him mad with passion because he doesn't waste any time mounting her and plunging deep inside. He grabs her waist and bucks into her with quick, darting motions. Again, I fear the length of him will stab her on the inside and come up and out her throat! Though watching him penetrate her, I can't help but be consumed with the thought that maybe it was *he* who had never lain with anyone. He certainly doesn't seem like he has! His body jerks around like he is barely in control—as if he has completely surrendered to the sensation of the pleasure without a thought to the *feeling* of it all and making it last for as long as possible.

Poor Sorcia! She looks bored. Unimpressed. And most of all—uncomfortable. It's obvious she gets no enjoyment from this union. I know *I* could do a better job satisfying her than he can.

Don't do it, Blodwyn, Arik admonishes when the thought pierces through my mind.

Why not? I answer. *And how do you know what I'm going to do?*

Blodwyn! His voice rings sharply, but I wave my hand dismissively in the air.

It's already done.

In a moment of sentimental sisterhood, I whip up an impromptu spell. One of slithering satisfaction in my friend's time of need. I call upon my serpents to aid in the coupling of the witch and the wanderer.

The white, slippery body slithers from behind a rock in the room, travels up the side of the bed and over to the bodies in their animalistic position. Gently, he crawls up the side of Sorcia's leg. She tenses up for a second at the feeling but dismisses it as Michael's hand groping her. He shudders when she tenses her sex around his organ and continues to pound away at her. The serpent moves languidly, stealthily up her thigh and on the underside of her buttocks. The forked tongue flicks at her flesh, tickling her, making her writhe with little jolts of pleasure. He searches for her opening. Michael's small manhood leaves a space

Chapter Thirteen

that begs to be filled—a dripping gap dying to be plugged up.

With one swift motion, the serpent enters her, right in time and motion as Michael. Her eyes widen, her expression changes, and she cries out in ecstasy and surprise from the thickness of the snake's body forcing itself into her. She grunts and moans and gyrates her hips at the new sensation—one that makes her feel complete and on the edge of excitement. Michael notices not the intruder and assumes that Sorcia's sudden change in demeanor is from something that *he* did. This thought quickens his pace, heightens his pleasure, and he empties his seed deep and hard into her with wild bucks and grunts and groans.

But the snake still moves within. It grinds on her soft insides with Michael's depleted organ on its back—slowly, gently, back and forth, hitting all the necessary spots to bring her to completion. He thinks she moves her hips because she's savoring the last of his performance, but then she screams—driven to the edge with the ultimate explosion.

"Oh my God!" he gushes breathlessly. "You were so... so..." he stammers again, unable to find the words, unable to verbalize the orgasm that still shakes through his core. "I didn't hurt you, did I?"

"Uh... no," she whispers.

"You felt so good," he moans, and Sorcia scoots her body forward releasing him from sex.

177

And as Michael pulls himself out, the serpent wriggles its way out too and slithers back down the side of the bed to the rock from whence it came.

Michael jumps up and scrambles for his clothes. He screams something about evil and the devil and a curse. Something about devil worshipers and deception. He flails his body around, scrambling for his clothes, shouting in the tongue of my people and his native language. But I scarcely hear what he says—I only pick up on bits and pieces for Arik and I both go into a fit of uncontrollable laughter, and the sound of that quickly consumes my ears. Our laughter against the backdrop of his frantic movements is quite the sight to behold, and I double over with pains in my side from laughing so hard.

Chapter Fourteen

In the Time of Darkness
In the Age of Ice
Summertime, 673 AD
Caverns in the Far North
Afternoon of the Waning Gibbous Moon

Aizel and Trond hear my fit of hysterics and make their way to the pillar where I hide. "Blodwyn?" Aizel inquires when she sees me doubled over. "Blodwyn, are you okay? What are you doing here?" She's puzzled. Concerned. Trond's pale face darkens with suspicion at my mirth, and I straighten up and calm myself down.

"It's nothing, nothing," I rattle, desperately trying to control myself, yet knowing my smile is still plastered on my face.

"What's going on?" Aizel asks.

I smooth out the front of my pinafore and inhale deeply to muster up my composure. "I said nothing. Arik was sharing a joke with me, that's all." I bend down slightly and rustle up the top of Trond's blond hair. "Just a joke. A silly adult-joke that little ears wouldn't fully understand. In fact, I don't think I understood it either, but it just tickled me something awful! Hit my funny bone hard."

Trond smiles at me. "I know what you mean. Sometimes silly things are just funny," he says so innocently.

I nod and give him a quick wink. "So true and so wise, Ruz."

But Aizel eyes me coolly. "Blodwyn?" she sings, dragging out the sounds of the letters.

I put an arm around each of them and begin walking them back over to the altar when, suddenly, Michael and Sorcia come racing through the corridor of the cave in a whirlwind.

Sorcia grabs onto Michael's arm and throws herself to the ground in hysterics. "No! Please don't leave! You said you would stay. You promised you would stay longer! We still have so much more to do!"

Aizel and I look at each other skeptically, and I reach my arm over Trond's shoulder to pull him closer to me.

Michael shakes Sorcia loose with rage and fury. His dark eyes dart around the room until he finds me, Aizel and Trond huddled together by the altar. "Devil worshipers!" he spits. "Unclean, unholy practices take place here. You're all deceivers and agents of the devil in a place where the serpent resides. The serpent is the conduit of the devil, Sarah. I told you that so many times. And she..." he shouts and points at me. Trond's body shakes from the shock of it. "She is beyond redemption. She is the devil's concubine!"

"No! Michael, please! It's not like that!" Sorcia begs, and her pathetic voice sends shockwaves up my arms. *I could kill her for her weakness...* "Blodwyn, tell him! Tell him of the good we do!"

I tighten my lips together trying to remain calm. "I don't know what you want me to say, Sorcia. He's not a prisoner here. He's our guest. If he wants to leave..."

"Sorcia," he growls. "The devil's name. I gave you a new one. A holy one. Yet your people don't recognize that, do they?"

Sorcia stands and again grips his arm tightly. "You said it yourself, it could take some time to get the others to see things your way. Years, even. Please. I beg you. If there is any feeling for me in your heart, stay! If you have any love for me, don't go!"

"I can't stay here in this place of evil, Sarah. I saw things in this place that I never thought possible. Evil things. Awful things. I am convinced that there is no salvation here. It is obvious to me that no matter how hard I try, progress cannot be made in this cave. I need to go, and I am offering you ... come back with me. I do care about you and your eternal soul, and you know my people will welcome you with open arms. You've made so much progress, and we still have work to do. Good work. Important work. But I cannot stay in this place of death and malice any longer."

In the cave light, I see the tears flowing down Sorcia's cheeks. Tears of conflict. They make her face glisten and shimmer and make her dark eyes shine with a glossy veneer. She looks unhuman—like a watery goddess about to dissolve into her own tears. She looks to me and Trond and Aizel, then back to Michael with her round, wet eyes. The gloss of the tears tries to mask the darkness within them, but it's still there—the darkness piercing the light. Trond's body tenses up against mine. Too young to understand the magnitude of what is unfolding before him, yet old enough to understand this moment is important. I pull him in closer to me as we three wait with bated breath for Sorcia's response.

She sighs and looks lovingly at Michael. Her eyes plead with him—*please*. He stares back at her, and his eyes seem to be saying the same thing. He *does* care for her. He wants to help her—to save her. To bring her fully and completely into his world.

"I... I..." she stammers.

A collective breath holds itself in the cave. Aizel grabs my hand.

"I can't go with you, Michael," she says reluctantly, her voice quivering with doubt.

He shakes her off him one last time. "Then, you've made your choice. If you ever change your mind, you know where I'll be." He glares hard at me one last time before turning from Sorcia and exiting the cave.

Sorcia falls to the ground again in a heap. Her black hair strewn across the rocky floor, and her muffled wails echo throughout the cavern. Quickly, we rush to her side and kneel beside her. Aizel gathers her hair and lays it down her back, stroking her gently to calm her down. "Don't cry, Sorcia," Trond's sweet little voice tries to coax. "Don't cry. We're here for you."

Aizel and I smile at each other, and I reach for his hand to assure him he's comforting her properly. I am amazed by his kindness and empathy, for it is in such stark contrast to my own blunt and abrasive demeanor.

He is still but a child, Aizel says to my mind. *You were once as sweet as he.* I roll my eyes and shake my head at her. Modir would have said otherwise. It is known that I was a hellchild with an explosive temper, and most of Modir's teachings to me involved isolating my anger and directing that energy to do my will. "Temper, temper brings the tempest," she would say. I never understood it back then, but as I got older it became clearer. Trond isn't like that. He doesn't have the spark of rage that I do. But maybe that's the way it needed to be? He is the light, and I am the dark?

Or maybe he will eventually grow into his own hot emotions? Aizel says silently to me, and I nod.

Sorcia's cries quiet down to quick-breath huffs. "There you go; there you go," Aizel sings as she pats her back a few more times.

Slowly, Sorcia turns her body over, and her black eyes stare at me with a desolate, faraway look to them. Like she's gone. Like she's lost. Like she's not herself. "Why didn't you help me?" she asks, and her voice is so hollow and weak it scarcely sounds like her.

"How, Sorcia? How should I have helped you?" I reply.

"Why didn't you make him stay? You could have made him stay. You have the power, Blodwyn. You made Ylfa stay…"

"Eh, eh," Aizel makes a clicking-like noise in her throat that cuts off Sorcia's sentence. Sorcia looks to Aizel, knowingly bows her head, then looks back to me.

"You know what I mean," she continues. "You could have helped me, Blodwyn. I love him."

"I couldn't force him to stay, Sorcia. He was a guest in our home. He ate our food, drank our wine. The Law of Abode would have prevented me from keeping him here."

She hangs her head again, so her hair covers her face. "But he was mine," she weeps. "I finally had something that was mine."

From the corner of my eye, I see a wave of worry darken Aizel's face. I pretend like I don't notice, but I also can't deny Sorcia's words made me a little uneasy as well.

"Don't be silly," Aizel says, trying to keep her tone light and airy. "He's just a man, Sorcia. There are plenty of others out there. With your beauty and charm, it won't be long before another takes his place!"

Chapter Fourteen

Aizel gives a nervous giggle, but Sorcia doesn't make a sound. Instead, she bends her legs to her chest and rests her face on her knee tops. "He was mine," she whispers with a low growl. "I finally had something that was mine."

Like an explosion, I shoot up from the floor and straighten out upright. It takes everything I have to not unleash my anger and fury at her pathetic display. I want to shout at her that she's weak and useless and has always been an outsider! My flesh burns as if I'm on fire. The tattoos scream red and orange, and the empty spaces between the runes are charred black. I can smell it. *They* can smell it too. Singed hair and burnt skin. Afraid my clothes will catch fire, I slip my cloak from my shoulders, and it drops to the ground. There's a weight in the center of my chest. It pulsates and resonates throughout my entire body—lifting me up and off the ground. I am off the ground! I look down and realize that I hover a few inches from the floor—I hover above the others who are on their knees and huddled before me. Trond's eyes go wide, and he squeaks out, "Blodwyn?" but I can't tell if he says it in his head or if he says it out loud. Aizel throws her arms around him and pulls him into her. There's a song in the distance. A dissonant tune created by voices from another time and place—another realm. I've heard this song before. It fills me so completely and propels me higher off the ground. I clench my fist and every torch in the cave ignites.

Trond jolts against Aizel, and she whispers words of comfort into his ear.

"Lest you not forget the extent of your own power, Sorcia," I say. But it's not my voice. Not really. I am overcome with the voice of the ancients. They speak to me, in me, through me. I hear them whisper in my head, yet it is I who forms the words. I am theirs, and they are mine. We are becoming one. Floating. Shifting. Transforming.

Sorcia tries to speak, tries to respond, but her words are silenced in her throat. Her words are silenced in her mind—for the moment a thought forms, I snatch it with my celestial hand and toss it into the brazier by the altar. Her words are runes above her head—and I snuff them out before they have a chance to be born.

"There is nothing you can say," I say, but my voice is a growl, a cacophony of hundreds of sounds and voices singing out all at once.

In me.

Through me.

She thinks the name *Grom,* and I hold it in my hand for a few moments before burning it.

"Grom—he who would destroy our family. Michael—he who would change you into something you are not. Yes, I did help you, Sorcia. I helped you see the error of your ways." In a flash, I project images to her of what could have been— images of Grom alerting the Jarl about how we buried Modir. Images of the hunting party coming out to our lands and digging up her body.

Images of us being put to the stake—baby Trond included. One by one, I bombard her mind with visions of the horrific consequences each one of her lovers would have inflicted upon us—all of us! Like lightning, they flash behind her eyes and rock her body with electric jolts until she finally throws her hands in the air and yells, "Enough! Enough! No more! I beg you!"

Gently, I float back to the rocky ground and kick the loose stones underneath my feet. Poor Trond! He has completely hidden himself within Aizel's body and he trembles with fear. *Be not afraid*, I say to his mind. *Just keep your good thoughts flowing. I would never hurt you.* Reluctantly, he pokes his head out from her armpit and looks to me. I give a small grin, and his body relaxes.

"I see. I see," Sorcia relents.

"Aye."

"I'm still here. This is home. I know that."

"Aye."

Sorcia stands up and meets me face to face. "Thank you, Blodwyn. Thank you for always helping me. In your own way, you do. Sometimes it's just hard to see." And she kisses me on the cheek and walks to the long corridor back to her area in the cave.

Trond rushes over to me and fiercely wraps his arms around my waist. "I know. I know," I say petting the top of his head lovingly. "Everything is fine now. You know I would never hurt you, right? You know my job is to always protect you, right?"

"Right," he replies sheepishly, and the heat of his breath radiates down the side of my leg.

But his small response gives me a moment to pause. "What? You don't believe me?"

"I do," he answers, again, directly into my leg so that his voice is muffled. "I promise."

Aizel glares at me with a look of consternation. "What happened, Blodwyn? What was that all about?"

"Arik caught the two of them together, and I thought I'd have a little fun. I guess it bothered Michael so much that…"

Come to think of it, where are you, Arik?

"No. I mean with *you*. What you just did. It was…"

"Unreal," Trond interrupts.

"I don't really know," I say. "I was completely overwhelmed. No, that's not the right word. It was more like being filled up. Like there were these empty places inside me that I never really noticed before and all at once they were complete."

"You changed," Trond says.

I look at Aizel quizzically, and she nods. "You rose off the ground. And it was still you, but it wasn't."

"Hmmm," I muse. "I… I don't really know…"

Trond suddenly picks up his head and looks at Aizel. Her eyebrows furrow, and her lips tighten together forming a thin line. I'm confused at first by the sudden gestures, but then quickly realize he's communicated with her again without me hearing it. I unlatch Trond's arms from my waist and hold him at arm's length. "What is it?" I say frantically to him. I look up at Aizel and ask her the same. "What? What's going on?"

"Did Sorcia say anything before she went back to her room?" Aizel asks.

"Right after she kissed me? No. Why?"

Aizel narrows her eyes at Trond. "Are you sure?"

Trond nods, his head of white bobs up and down furiously.

"I didn't hear her say anything either, but Trond says he heard Sorcia say…"

Energy begins to rise within me. I can't pinpoint exactly what the emotion is, though. Anger? Jealousy? Sadness? I didn't hear him, just like when I overheard the two of them talking before. There was that moment of silence between them, and I knew they were communicating. My own brother shut me out! Was it done purposefully, or is it a part of his abilities that he has yet to control? "Wait! What do you mean 'Trond says?' Trond didn't *say* anything just now! What are you two keeping from me?"

"Oh, stop it, Blodwyn!" Aizel scolds. "You know he's still coming into his own! Besides, you're not one to walk around with your pride hurt in that way! That's not you."

I suck in my emotions with a deep breath and calm myself. "Continue," I say on exhale. "What did Trond hear Sorcia say?"

"She's going to leave, Blodwyn. She's going to go to Michael and his people, and she's going to leave *us*."

I grab Trond's shoulder and spin him to face me. "Is this true? This is what you heard her say?"

He nods. "She said it in her head. Right after she kissed you. She said she would be going to Michael as soon as she got a chance."

"You heard her from inside?" I ask, tapping my temple with my forefinger.

He nods again.

"No worries, Ruz. Sometimes when the moon is darkest, the light inside takes over and illuminates what can't be seen."

"She was able to shut her thoughts off to us, but she probably didn't anticipate Trond picking up on it," Aizel says.

I take a deep breath and call out to Arik with my astral voice, but he doesn't answer.

Why doesn't he answer?

"If she wants to leave, she can leave," I say with an exaggerated exhale.

Aizel's eyes go wide. "No, Blodwyn! She... she can't!"

"She's not a prisoner, Aizel. None of us are. We're all free to be whom we want and go where we want."

"Blodwyn! You know it's not that simple. Who knows what Michael's group is capable of. Or what deal they made with the Jarl."

I shake my head. "Oh, I know," I respond matter-of-factly. "I said she's free to go, but that doesn't mean she will. This is the only life she's ever really known. She won't leave it. She won't leave us. She's too afraid to... she's too afraid of *me* to leave." With that I bend down, give Trond a peck on the top of his head and make my way out of the cave.

"Where are you going?" Aizel calls to my back.

"Out. In the forest. I need to think."

Chapter Fifteen

In the Time of Darkness
In the Age of Ice
Summertime, 673 AD
The Frostheim Forest of the Far Northlands
Night of the Waning Gibbous Moon

The glow of the waning moon is bright against the black inky sky. Just the side of her is darkened by the transitioning process like a chunk of her has been bitten off. The stars twinkle and blink and occasionally something astral in the distance darts across the dark expanse leaving its tail of shimmer in its wake. I stretch my body out on my side—right next to Modir's grave—and curl one leg over the subtle hump of disturbed soil much like I do when I sleep next to Arik and burrow myself in his arms and body. "There are so many stars out tonight," I say out loud to Modir. "More than ever if I had to guess. You would have loved this. It's a beautiful night."

I know she won't answer. She never does. It's been seven years, and I can barely feel her presence anymore.

"I wish you could see Trond. I wish you could be here for him. He has great power for a boy his age. He scares me sometimes—the things he says, the things he does, the things he knows. Sorcia, Aizel, and I are going to have to tread lightly around that one!" I laugh a gentle laugh. "He's delightful. Happy. I love him deeply. You would be so proud. No child should be without their mother."

A wind blows through, and I shiver with an overwhelming feeling of not being at home. I don't feel like I'm home—like, I'm here in this place of my mother's burial, I have the conscious awareness that *yes, I am in fact present in the Frostheim*, but there's a strangeness looming around me that I can't quite pinpoint. The crisp night air, the glimmer of the heavens, and this... this silence that invades the space around me feels oddly out of place, yet oddly familiar, like I've been swept off to somewhere else. Somewhere peaceful.

Suddenly, I stop and recognize my thoughts. *Silence*.

I've never really had a *silent* moment in all my life. There have always been voices, or music, or my own inner dialogue, and for the last seven years—Arik. There has always been *something* going on in my head. But now? There's just me. If I stop thinking, there will be nothing. Silence! Just close my eyes and...

"Ahhh," I exhale. That felt good! A quiet reprieve. If just for one minute. If just for one fleeting moment in time. It was nice. I wonder if that's what it sounds like right before death—when everything in the world around you inhales and holds its breath, and then the quiet washes over you, and you're free.

"Is that what you felt, Modir?" I say, patting the grass above her grave. "Is that what you heard? Did the quiet come over you when you left us? Is that why you smiled? Was that your moment of peace and release?"

The grass is greener on her mound like the soil knew her essence—sucked it in and sprouted forth the most verdant swath of land in the entire forest. Modir is alive and well! My efforts to bring her back to physical form may have failed, but the ground knows—the earth knows. Her magic and spark settled deep in the roots of this land and spread forth her essence throughout the forest. She's here with me now—in the trees, in the leaves, in the yellow and white petals of the sweet summer daisies. I breathe her in every moment of every day, and I just don't realize it.

"But I do realize it!" I say as I sit up on my side. "I do! If I didn't feel you, would I even entertain these one-sided conversations?" I chuckle at the thought.

I chuckle to myself.

At myself.

Because if I don't laugh, I'll cry.

I sit up on my bottom and look at the field around me. For the first time, I really take it in. Maybe it's the moon, and the stars, and the rotating waves of silence that make me look at my surroundings with a clear mind, but I notice that Modir's gravesite is lush—teeming with all kinds of life. And the colors are so vibrant around it. The colors of the wildlife sing songs and tell tales, and fight against the muted colors of the rest of the woods so as to be noticed and honored and revered. As if they are saying, "Here lies the Blodheksa."

And in that moment—in that color-swirled, open-eyed, revelation—I hear Modir's voice from long ago say, "Everything above ground is dormant. Everything below ground grows."

I look up to the waning moon and remember her teachings for planting and harvesting and how everything needed to be in accordance with the cycles of the lunar being.

"Everything below ground grows," I say in a low whisper.

When the moon wanes.

"Everything below ground grows," I say louder, like the pieces are all falling into place.

Planting time for things that have seeds inside.

"Seeds inside! Inside!" I scream. I don't know why, but that's the first thing that comes out. Saying the words just felt right.

Piercing through the silence and my moontide revelation, I am suddenly rocked with flashes of light behind my eyes that throw me off balance and leaves me dizzy. The sides of my head throb in rhythm with my heartbeat—an invasion I know all too well, but never at this magnitude. Arik calls out to me with such urgency I must blink my eyes for a few moments until the speckles dissipate back into the darkness. Quickly, I tune my inner vision into his astral wave and see through him (for it's become a natural function, like swallowing, or breathing and can be done at will).

He's tracking someone in the darkness, staying a few steps behind them in the woods. They reach a clearing, and I get a whiff of salt water on the cool breeze. People mill about the alleyways, fires burn in the hearths of the homes, candles glow in windowsills, and unfolding before me out of the darkness and into the shadowy light, Sorcia sneakily slides her body up to the front door of a familiar structure. By the way she looks over her shoulder, it's apparent she suspects she's been followed. She knocks three times with a deliberate beat, the door flies open, and an arm reaches out and whisks Sorcia in. The figure then steps into the threshold, looks around to make sure she's alone, and follows him inside.

It's Michael. Trond was right in what he heard. Sorcia left us.

What do you want me to do? Arik asks.

But I don't respond. I can't. Physically, I can't verbalize my wants and needs. Psychically, I am paralyzed. My breath. My breath. It's labored and quick. I gulp in air, yet it doesn't fill my lungs. I gasp. *I breathe in deep and hard yet find it difficult to catch my breath. I choke on the panic in my chest and pant and gulp for air.*

Sorcia left us. I can't believe she left us, I mutter to Arik on the inside.

Chapter Fifteen

Yes, Blodwyn. I know.

I never thought she would... or she could... or she...

You know why, Blodwyn. You just need to breathe now. Breathe.

I am frozen, and a tumult of emotion comes crashing over me. Giant tears swell at the bottoms of my eyes making my vision jagged and fuzzy. They are so jagged that I could tear open the sky with just a mere glance and open the gateway to let the old ones flood in and destroy the earth. Large globules of my anguish rise and cascade down my cheeks. These tears are thick, weighty... so heavy they feel like they will pull my bottom eyelids down to my chin.

The dichotomy of anger and despair are at war in my heart and in my mind. It's a familiar mix of rage and sadness. I've known this feeling before. I've felt this feeling before...

And then it hits me.

Modir.

This feeling is so familiar because it's exactly how I felt the night she died. Betrayal, anger, sadness, loss, uncertainty, confusion, yet knowing, and everything in between. My tattoos glow orange, and skin singes again. I collapse onto Modir's gravesite, and the heat of me tarnishes the green grass. The brown outline of my body is emblazoned in the ground, as I pound both fists on the soil trying to punch my way through.

"Why did you leave me?" I scream to Modir's corpse within. "Why did you go?"

But I suspect the inquiry is for both Modir and Sorcia, for the feelings are parallel.

"I can't do this without you! First, you leave me with Trond with no guidance. Now there's a traitor in my midst! I don't know what to do. *You* would know what to do! *You* always knew what to do! Tell me what I need to do!"

My forceful blows make imprints in the soil—the grass disturbed by my fire and rage. And again, the flood of enormous tears spring from my eyes. Tears the likes of which I have never seen. They flow cold against my fever-hot face, and they gather into miniature puddles on the blades of upset grass beneath me.

"I miss you, Mother. I ache for you," I weep long and hard into the soil, emptying every speck of emotion that had been building up since the day she died.

The air shifts direction, but I pay it no mind. I hear a drum beat off in the distance, but I ignore that as well for I have opened the floodgates, the deep well of feeling that had been closed off all this time.

I realize that during all these years, I was so concerned with bringing Modir back, that I hadn't truly processed that she was gone. It's not that I hadn't recognized her absence, it's just that there was always something to preoccupy me and shove the reality of her death into the back of my consciousness—Trond, my commitment to the circle, Ylfa, Arik (oh, yes, Arik…), my serpent birth, Grom, the Jarl, now Michael and the missionaries—there has always been something to force me to close off my feelings. To sever myself and put up my walls. To make it less real.

And I never fully acknowledged how much it hurt.

A sick wave lurches my stomach forward, but nothing is released. I cough on my pain, my guilt, and my despair. I choke on it because the words took so many years to develop on my lips, and I am ashamed. Ashamed of myself and for not recognizing it sooner...

I love you, Mother. I loved you then, and I love you still.

I'm sorry.

Michael's words come back to me—*Jesus wept*, and in an instant, I understand. I see it so very clearly: Jesus wept hard and true tears for the loss of one of his best friends—the death of the one called Lazarus. His sadness was so deep and raw that the very tears that fell upon the dirt floor of Lazarus's tomb shook the earth beneath as it sprang forth with new life. Reborn. The truth of Jesus's suffering was the almighty transformative power to *create*.

Everything below ground grows.

Because Jesus wept.

Lazarus lived again because Jesus wept.

Now, I weep. Deep, painful tears. Desperate tears. My heart feels like it will burst through my chest. And as I empty the essence of my heavy soul onto the soil, a song echoes from the distance. It's low at first, and I suspect it's been there in the background for some time, but it's noticeably louder now — rumbling not only in my mind but out there amongst the trees. The insects and animals stir as the sound of it rises and penetrates every fiber of every being.

I close my eyes and listen. It's the song I've grown so accustomed to — the one with the discordant voices singing in the ancient tongue and the slow and steady rhythm of the drums *thump, thump, thump*. But something has changed — something is different. I isolate the voices in my mind's eye as if I'm separating one unharmonious sound from the next. I sift through the different tones and noises until I recognize a voice — a singular, melodic voice singing out above the rest.

Modir.

I hear her! Clear as day! Her voice is carried on the summer night breeze, and it fills my heart and displaces my sadness. She's there! She's here! Out in the cosmos and here in the clearing with me. She calls out. Sings the song of the old ones. I hear it! I hear her!

But then, another voice overpowers her, and I twist and turn my head struggling to make sense of it before I perceive it to be the sounds of an old god. Evanak. She sings in low tones with a gurgling voice like there is a fresh spring of water churning in her throat. But I hear her! She is with Modir. And she is now with me.

One by one, all the voices detach themselves from the chorus and make themselves known. Thousands of heksas from ages past — the old ones, monsters from the birth of time. They cry to me to do their will. *Free us, free us from our celestial prison!* To them, I am their last bastion of hope.

Thousands of heksas from a time more familiar to me—battle-weary witches from sands and snow cheering me on to complete my task. Contemporaries of Modir. Modir herself. They are all together in a rallying cry. Their voices are the loudest as they are the closest to me in the timeline of the now.

Thousands of heksas from a time far away—a future unknown with crows and steel contraptions. Their voices are fainter than my elders of yore, but they are present nonetheless. I am in awe at how they reach across space and time and sing with our brethren. They look fuzzy, transparent in my mind's eye, and it's hard to discern their countenances. So many of them—black-haired beauties cutting down a circle of their enemies in the woods, brown-haired maidens tied to burning stakes, pious women taking vows and pledges, mysterious maidens scrying over bowls of water in a makeshift tent with twinkling lights like stars (but not) all around them. So many in service to the cause. So many to rise after my time. I don't know how far down the line of twilight I can perceive, but their voices tell me they are strong and crafty, and they are close, oh so very close. I am there with them, yet it isn't me. Not my body in the form that I am familiar with, but my *fylgja* remains. I sing to myself. I hear my own raspy voice, like screaming down the hallway of a cave. She is me. I am her. I am many hers until I am one. I don't understand parts of the song, but it makes sense in my heart.

And the colors are so bright in the days of future come—blacks, and reds, and silvers, and violets, and golds swirl around a gash in the sky. A rip in the sky. A tear in the sky where the old ones will spill forth.

All of them. All of them heksas.

All of them call to me.

And I sway, and dance, and harness all their energy and combine it with my own. They have granted me this moment to draw them down—the multitude of them—and pull them into me.

Even though it is truly nighttime, for me, it is night no more. My eyes see every color, every spark, every essence, and every aura of every living thing in the space before me. The sky is alive as the stars shift and move. It is a violent dance of the heavens to herald the coming.

My coming.

My transformation.

My transcendence.

For I am Legion, and with the power of the heksas from past, present, and future, we rip through the fabric of time and space. We claw through the gash in the sky. We punch through the confines of our reality.

And finally wake up Modir.

Chapter Sixteen

In the Time of Darkness
In the Age of Ice
Summertime, 673 AD
The Frostheim Forest of the Far Northlands
Night of the Waning Gibbous Moon

Silence befalls the woods around me, and the ground beneath my feet rumbles. Trembles. It's not enough to shake mountains or topple structures, but it's jarring enough that the trees wobble at their roots from deep within the soil. A shuddering. A fluttering. Like something rising from the earth.

Someone.

Instinctively, I fall to my knees and dig with my bare hands. I pull up fistfuls of grass and dirt and toss them over my shoulder. In my hair, at the corners of my eyes—I breathe in the soil and let the strong earth scent fill my lungs. As I scoop handfuls upon handfuls from aboveground, my preternatural senses know for certain there's something underneath trudging through the dirt.

Trudging upward.

Clawing through the thick mound of earth that had been packed so neatly.

She is coming.

There is no doubt in my mind, no mistake in my heart. Modir is finally awake and desperately trying to free herself from her soil prison.

A shock of euphoric joy makes my heart leap in my chest. I physically gasp for air at the thought of Modir's return! How I've longed for this day. Prayed for this day. Made offering upon offering, said the words, and performed countless rituals all for this day. It has finally come. I thought I was prepared for this moment, but I am no more prepared for her resurrection than I was for her passing. There's an anxiety and apprehension that mixes with my utter happiness—it swirls in a dangerous maelstrom in the center of my chest. Oh, but I can't wait to fling myself into her arms, bury my face in the crook of her neck, inhale the scent of her long, red hair, and tell her how much I have missed her.

I've missed you so much, Modir. But we will be together now, for always.

For all ways.

My tattoos burn hot on my flesh, and that propels me to speed up my actions. I feel like I've barely made any progress, so I pick up my pace and dig faster. "Sky above me, earth below me, fire within me," I chant using my cupped hands to shovel through the ground. Arik had dug this grave seven years ago on my orders, and I instructed him to dig it as deep as he possibly could so that no one would be the wiser of a body here. "Sky above me, earth below me, fire within me." But now, I fear my instructions were wrong. What if Modir is struggling underneath and doesn't make it out in time? "Sky above me, earth below me, fire within me." What if Modir is struggling so hard that she gives up and returns to her earthen resting place?

I can't let that happen!

Faster and deeper still—at a panicked, frantic pace, I dig and heave, dig and heave.

"Seven years!" I scream, and I am suddenly overcome with a sense of dread.

Modir has been in the ground for seven years.

Seven.

I know all too well the way time ravages a body, especially one that is deceased. Time is unforgiving. Cruel. And as much as I like to romanticize Modir's return with her woman form intact and her silky red hair fixed to perfection, I am struck with the hard-handed reality—there is a possibility of Modir being different, of Modir being *changed*.

I scan my mind for what Michael said about Lazarus and how Jesus raised him from the dead. I can't recall if Michael mentioned how Lazarus looked, but I do remember him saying Jesus worked his miracle within days of Lazarus's passing. Maybe I'm too late? Maybe Modir is too far gone? Maybe she cannot release herself from the ground because she is but a bag of bones with fingers that can only scrape away the dirt? Maybe she no longer has eyes to see, and the soil fills the open sockets of her skeletal face every time she tries to move her head to the surface?

The ground beneath me shudders right in time with my shuddering on the inside.

I shudder.

With fear.

That's not something I normally do, for *I* am the one who *brings* the fear.

But I am frozen with it right now and questioning everything I ever thought to be the truth and the way. Is it possible I've made a mistake? Is it possible I've been wrong all this time? The thought of my mother as an animated figure of bones had never crossed my mind. The thought of my mother as a walking shell of decayed flesh wasn't ever a possibility in my brain. Until now.

The rumbling from the ground grows louder, and as I look down at the hole I've carved out on my side of the world, there's movement in the dirt. Real, actual, visible movement—like a hand slithering its way up from the underbelly of the world.

I shut my eyes tight. "Please!" I beg no one in particular. "Don't let it come through!" Because I don't think I can live with myself if I see Modir as nothing but the way she was the day I committed her to the earth.

The ground quivers again, and I hear the dirt fling upward from below and scatter onto the grass. I can bear it no more. I so desperately want to turn on my heels and race back to the cave, but

I know I can't. I know I must face what I have summoned, regardless of how ghastly it may be.

I take a step back and press myself against a tree trunk. Never once do I open my eyes, yet in my mind the scene unfolds clearly. My brain takes note of the sounds and smells and fashions the images of my imagination. But it's not my imagination, not really. Behind my closed eyelids, I can *see*.

Up from the disturbed dirt of Modir's grave, hands punch through and gangly arms spring out from below, bent, and thin like spider legs. Skeletal hands grip the sides of the opening and hoist a body-figure through the void. A body-figure made of bones with the remnants of rotted flesh dangling from it. My stomach drops when it emerges—wriggles its torso aside the grave and uses its elbows as leverage to lift the lower portion of itself up and out.

Up and out.

How can this be? It's been so long, yet her hair holds the same blazing red color.

I must look. I must see. There is a part of me that is curious to physically witness what has spewed forth from the earth. When I do, tears uncontrollably stream down my face as I am met with the pitiful sight of this reanimated corpse writhing on the ground before me.

"Oh, Modir," I say to the pathetic mass of bones. "What have you become?"

It breaks my heart as the body-figure twists and turns itself in inhuman ways—its boney frame juts in different directions that defies all laws of mankind. Again, I find it strange that it even has any cohesion and mobility at all in this almost-skeletal state, so I kneel to get a closer look. The face of it is still somewhat intact—patchy skin blackened with rot hangs from the cheek area, a gaping hole for a nose, yet the eyes of the thing have been preserved but glossed over with the white film of death. It opens its jaw as if to speak, but there is nothing there to produce sound. Just the hollow, transparency of old and decayed tissue and the silence of the being sends a chill in my body because I know it wishes to speak, but it can't, yet it still tries.

The figure struggles as it tries to drag itself toward me, its bones scrape along the grass and leave a scar in the ground as it moves along. Green blades crunch and flatten underneath the weight of the creature. For a second, I think it reaches its arm out to point in my direction, and I wince in disgust and dismay.

This is not what I wanted.

This is not what I wanted.

This is not what…

But its arm is extended still—reaching for me, beckoning to me as it continues its struggle to advance forward using one arm.

Surely Lazarus was not in such a dire state.

"Easy, Modir," I say calmly to it. "It's me. Blodwyn." I put my arm out toward it like you would do to placate a wild animal, and its eyes widen with even more determination to reach me.

Chapter Sixteen

I panic. My heart beats faster and my runes glow brightly. I second-guess everything I've done the last seven years. But when the body finally reaches me, all doubt and fear wash away, for when the tip of the skeleton finger touches mine, it's as if an explosion goes off inside my head. With one last heave toward me, Modir wraps her bone fingers tightly around my wrist and we are connected as a blanket of light envelopes us. The tattoos sing out in red and orange, and my entire body throbs with pulsing light. It is so beautiful! She shows me images of the other realms. She takes me beyond time and space — much like how I guided Michael on the vision quest, but this is somehow much larger in scope, and by far more intense. Modir walks me through death. And death is a valley of fire. And in that fire, all are cleansed. All are reborn into the new and everlasting covenant.

Soon, the light from my tattoos penetrates the figure's bones, and in a swirl of hazy fog, it is rebuilt. She is *rebuilt*. Rejuvenated. Sinew and muscle and skin begin to take shape again on her body. Reassembled so that she looks more like the Modir from my memory and less like a ghastly draugr come to life. Just as she gave of herself to bring me into this world, she takes life from me to reshape her again. She is transformed, yet not the same, like there is still more work to be done. She takes just enough of me that she can stand; however, I am so drained of life, that I collapse to the ground in an ironic reversal of roles. Modir ceases the transference of energy, turns from me to exit the forest, and leaves me at her gravesite.

Because she needs more to be complete.

I try to get up and follow, but I am too weak and dizzy and unsteady on my feet. I know exactly where Modir is headed, and I certainly can't let Trond see her this way. With the last bits of energy I have, I send a message to Aizel with my mind's astral eye: *Get Trond away from the cave. Modir is coming.* I pray hard she hears me.

And just as Modir struggled to drag herself across the ground, I find it hard to right myself and move. It feels like a lifetime before I catch my bearings and head back to the cave. I know she has gotten there before me; I just hope Aizel and Trond were able to leave before she arrived.

When I enter the cave, it seems my prayers were answered, for they are nowhere in sight. In fact, there is no trace of them whatsoever—the torches and firepits have all been extinguished and a dark, sullen hush fills the halls. I imagine Aizel hurriedly snuffed out all the lights, whisked Trond under her cloak, and absconded into the night. The air in here is thick—heavy. It is oppressive with the aura that I am not alone. In the undercurrent of the silence, the sounds of someone breathing and shuffling deep within the cavern make themselves known to me.

Quickly, I make my way to Ylfa's chamber, but I am too late. The abomination that is Modir lurks behind the abomination that is Ylfa. Trapped in her own mind, Ylfa has no idea that anyone is even in the room with her. Her frail and fragile body slumps languidly in her chair as Modir places her hands on Ylfa's shoulders.

She intends to do her harm. "Modir!" I scold, and they both look up at me. Ylfa gives a small, knowing smile when she realizes I'm there, and Modir glares at me behind her wild, white-glazed eyes. There is something sinister to them, and for a second, I question if it's even my mother in that ghastly body of rot and ruin. "Modir?" I say again with a questioning lilt at the end of the word.

Something like a smirk creeps up the corner of Modir's mouth. *Oh, it's me, Blodwyn,* it says to me. Her silent voice is like a spray of ice water in my skull. It drips down the back of my neck and down my shoulders, and I physically shiver. But it's not her voice from my memory. It's laden with a crunching din that sounds neither human nor beast. Neither draugr nor sublime being. It scares me into awareness, and I brace myself for the unknown because I know I should be happy at this resurrection, but there is something so terribly wrong.

Modir bends forward into the crook of Ylfa's neck and clamps her mouth furiously down. Ylfa squirms from the shock and the pain of Modir's dull teeth breaking through the flesh. She chews her, gnaws her, grinds her jaw back and forth until Ylfa's blood spews uncontrollably into the rotted black cavern of Modir's mouth. Hungrily, she gulps and gurgles as she sucks down as much of Ylfa's blood as she can, but soon her mouth is overwhelmed with the substance, and it spills over Ylfa's shoulder like a waterfall. Dark red, like black in the darkness of the cave—in the blackness of the cave—but my color-filled vision sees it clearly, and the blood flows in a steady stream matting Ylfa's loose braid and staining her white pinafore dress.

Once again, Modir changes as she is filled with Ylfa's essence. Stronger still, her hands tighten on Ylfa's shoulders, holding her steady, locking her in place. When Ylfa's eyes close peacefully, I cry out, "Modir! Stop! No more!"

Modir's head snaps up, and Ylfa's blood sprays across the room and at my feet. She growls at me like an animal backed into a corner—feral and wild, and I scarcely wonder that in her blood-soaked stupor will she attack me next?

"She's gone," I say calmly, pointing at the dead girl in the chair. "It's not good to drink from the dead."

Modir eases her grip, and Ylfa's body slumps to ground with a *thud*. She stares at me with her cold eyes, and slowly I see the light behind them ignite. As if remnants of her former self are fighting to break through, fighting to rise to the surface and reclaim her body once again—reclaim the life she was torn away from. Her white eyes narrow in a pained expression, and she opens her mouth to say something, but a fountain of blood flows down her lower lip and chin and a gurgle sound hums in the back of her throat. The skin on her hands has completely regenerated, but there are still absent spaces of meat throughout the rest of her, like a speckled carcass picked apart by vultures.

"You need more, don't you?" I ask.

Another gurgle-sound from her hums in the cave.

Hums in my brain.

Hums in my heart.

But the sound is weary and painful, and I become dreadfully aware that she must be in agony. Locked between the world of the living and the world of the dead, her body and mind confused with what she knows and what she remembers.

Can you hear me? I say to her mind. *Do you know who I am?*

I think she nods, but it's such a subtle motion, I can't be sure.

"I brought you back, Modir. We need you. We need the Blodheksa."

Another gurgle sound followed by an agonizing moan, and my heart breaks again, for I understand that's not what she wants to hear. The thought of purpose and duty are the furthest things from her mind. The moan that came from her was one of pure suffering and distress.

"You need to ease your pain, don't you?" I say.

Modir's shoulders slump forward.

Suddenly, a thought overwhelms me. A thought that has always been there but has never had a chance to be realized. I still suffered from the betrayal of my former friend and companion.

Her allegiance to her god-fearing lover made a mockery of the years we spent together as a family. Sorcia had turned her back on every oath and every bond we had ever forged and standing here in Ylfa's room with the reanimated corpse of my beloved mother, it all seemed too easy—too perfect.

One by one, I flash scenes of the seaside town to Modir's mind, hoping she will see the barrage of images. I show her the structures, the center square, the docks, the people. I compartmentalize the images and show her Michael, and some of the faces of the members of his group that I remembered. I flash her an image of Sorcia and attach to it my feelings of unbridled rage and disgust.

"You know the town. You know the way," I instruct. "Go to them. Take them all. Ravage them all. *Kill* them all. They won't be able to stop you. Do as you will, and you'll feel better."

A glimmer shines in her eyes as they change from white to blue to green to gold and back to white. I step aside from the threshold of the room and motion for Modir to leave. She gurgles again, and this time it sounds like a giggle.

I can't help but giggle too.

Chapter Seventeen

In the Time of Darkness
In the Age of Ice
Summertime, 673 AD
Caverns in the Far North &
In the Village on the Outskirts of the Frostheim
Forest in the Far Northlands
All at once
Dawn of the Half Moon

A sinking feeling invades my stomach as Modir goes howling off into the forest as I wrestle with the thought: *Did I just bring my dead mother back to life and set her out to murder an entire village, including my former best friend?*

Yes. I believe I did. I can't help but smile. Modir will set right all the wrongs that have been done to us, and then she will be strong enough—herself enough—to rein as the supreme Blodheksa.

I know Arik is still in the village after having followed Sorcia there. I never told him to leave, so I call out to him and do my best to relay the events that have transpired—what I've done, and what he should expect to come his way shortly.

She is coming.

We instantly connect, and I see nothing but his vantage point. His excitement comes in colorful bursts of red and yellow, making the break of dawn so much more vivid and alive. I try to stifle his enthusiasm a little with images of how Modir looks with her sloughing, rotting flesh, her sunken in white-glazed eyes, and the blood and bile that spews from her mouth when she tries to communicate. All ghastly images that are not very Modir-like, and to be honest, that are quite disturbing. I try to caution his expectations, but her abhorrent visage only seems to make him even more delighted for her arrival.

I sit with my back against the wall of the cave and extend my arms at my sides. With the words of the ancients, I call to my children, and my den of white serpents slither to my side. They wrap their slinky bodies around my arms, absorbing the heat coming from my runes. Their flicking tongues tickle the spots of my exposed skin, and I am comforted by their presence. They adore me, worship me, and can't get enough of me, and they all show subtle signs of aggression as they fight for a position against my tattooed flesh. Some wriggle down my shirt and wrap themselves around my breasts. Others drape themselves around my neck and tangle their tails within the folds of my long braid. When they settle down, we feed from each other—a heksa and her familiars—my true children, born out of some ancient, primal force.

Our energies combine with Arik's so that we can all help guide Modir on her path. All of us together, all at once. We call upon the powers of the night to cloak Modir in darkness so as to not be seen by her victims. It is an ancient spell that is scarcely mentioned in all our oral history. It is dangerous, and heksas rarely use for it can quickly, and possibly fatally, drain the one who casts it, but it is the only chance I must fully and completely exact my revenge and restore Modir to her full capacity. I had always wondered why the old ones gifted me with the power of the serpents. Until now, I had never needed to call upon them for a cloaking ritual, and I surmise this has been the plan all along: if not for Arik's second sight, if not for the cunning of the snakes, if not for my own advanced power and strength, if not for this sacred dawning of the half-moon… The people of Michael's village are the sacrifices the gods demand, and I will have it no other way.

And Sorcia? Arik asks.

Sorcia most of all.

The destruction is at hand. And justice must be served. And blood must be spilled so Modir can live. And Modir must live to form the new world.

The people of the village are nestled dreamily in their beds—unaware of the danger that stealthily lurks in the early morning shadows. Unseen, unheard, Modir creeps in one by one and slashes throats and bludgeons skulls and decorates the walls of their pit houses with their red blood. Her hunger, her bloodlust, pulses so hot and strong that it takes me off guard and feels as if someone is standing on my chest. It gets harder for me to breathe each time she tears out someone's throat with her dull teeth or snaps someone's neck. Evisceration after evisceration, Modir plays with their innards, inspecting them like a child would before draping them across her face, taking the center part of the bloody rope into her mouth, and wagging her head back and forth so that the right and left side portions flail around the room like a knotted rope being tossed side to side. Arik is in ecstasy at the carnage left in Modir's wake. His pulse quickens. It throbs in my head in time with the throbbing sensation that suddenly springs up between my legs. If we were together right now, I know he would ravage me under the spray of intestinal blood. The snakes adorning my body make it impossible to satisfy myself, but that only intensifies the sensation.

Come home to me, Arik, my lustful mind calls to him.

There'll be plenty of time for that, he answers. *I must bring her back now. She's had her fill, and the cloak won't last much longer.*

Of course, the son of a seidr would know that!

Very well, I say, and as Arik calls Modir to him so they can make the journey home, the snakes let out a collective hiss. The sound of it mixed with the echoing screams of horror and confusion from the village fill my head with a new kind of song—the Love Song of Modir! It's a dark lullaby, a haunting tune of agony and ecstasy rolled into one.

Their massacre is the rebirth of the Blodheksa!

Oh, how they scream! For a split second, I am jealous that Arik had been so close to it all. I would have loved to have heard the dirge with my actual ears, but I'll have to settle for the astral wave of it. If the spell worked and Modir is healed and the missionaries are exterminated (and Sorcia and her foreigner lover are eliminated), then that is all that matters.

"Is everything in order now?" Aizel calls from the mouth of the cave.

I look up to see her with Trond clutching tightly to her waist. "I believe so," I answer. "Did you see…"

"Some," she says lowering her head.

"Most," Trond squeaks with a soft voice.

My heart sinks. The poor, sweet child. I wish he hadn't seen images of Mother like that. Not like that. Modir was beautiful and kind and powerful. That's how I want him to see her—to know her, not the shambling killer dancing in a fountain of blood. He looks to me with such a pained expression that I immediately feel the need to make things right. To explain. To calm his fears. *Because she was a horrific sight to behold.* "Brott!" I command the snakes to leave me in our ancient language, and in an instant, they slither from my body and back to their crevices in the cave. When I am free of them, I race to Trond and kneel before him. "Oh, Ruz," I sing, pushing his hair from his forehead. "Be not afraid. What happened in the village… what happened with Modir… it needed to be done. She needed to get better. You'll see. Arik is bringing her back right now. You'll see. It's going to be fine, now. Me, you, Aizel, Arik, Modir. The five of us will start a new life together. You'll see."

Trond forces a smile as thick tears form at the sides of his gray eyes. Aizel looks at me with grim consternation.

"What about Sorcia? And Ylfa?" he innocently coos.

"Don't worry about them. They're not coming with us."

"Why not?" he whines.

"They can't, Trond. It's not part of the plan. You need to keep your good thoughts flowing and…"

He snaps back away from my touch. "She killed them, didn't she," he says matter-of-factly as a scowl invades his face.

Aizel's eyes narrow and darken as if to say *don't confirm it,* but I ignore her plea and nod my head tersely.

"No! No!" he screams and jerks away from Aizel.

"Ruz! Please. When Arik and Modir get here…"

"I don't want to see her! I don't want to! She's not my mother!" And with that he goes racing out of the cave and into the forest.

"Ruz!" I call out and set my heels to chase after him.

Aizel puts her arm out to stop me. "No," she says. "I'll go get him. He's just a little boy. For as strong as he is, he's just a little boy."

I lower my head. "I've always told him the truth. I've never held anything back from him."

"But he saw, Blodwyn. He saw her. He saw what she did. He is going to need time to process it all."

"But they'll be here soon."

"Don't worry. I'll bring him when he's ready."

I nod to her in thanks as she leaves to follow him.

Guilt gnaws at me as I watch Aizel's figure disappear from the cave and out into the bright morning. None of this feels right—no matter how much I willed it so. Trond's face said it all, and the shame of what I've done makes my runes itch, like insects scurrying underneath my flesh. I violently run my fingernails up and down my arms to scratch the markings off me.

Just go away! I scream in my head. *Go back to where you came from! Leave my skin as it was. You don't need me to tell the tale—Modir has returned, and she can tell her own story again.*

But she can't. And I know it. And I am rocked with yet another wave of guilt.

One part of me is in awe of her—a living dead beauty walking the earth. My Modir! Swaying in the dawn's light neither here nor there. What secrets are locked away in her *fylgja*, and would she speak them if not for the black bile from her shredded throat? Can she tell me the mysteries of the hereafter even if she wanted to? Does she remember her time on this planet as well as her time in the ether?

I've waited for her return for so long and am thrilled that I was successful in my spell. Maybe that is the part I am most enamored with—my ability to rip her out from the great beyond after years of planning and plotting and practicing. I did it! I *did* it! I can't deny, the power emboldened me, strengthened me, made me feel like I was part of this world. It was an energy surge that still runs hot even after being weakened by the cloaking spell. There's an underlying pulse that makes me... different. Better.

And then, there is a part that is frightened beyond belief of Modir and of myself—how the living corpse devoured Ylfa and took so readily to my plan. I gave the command, gave her the order to massacre an entire community of people for my own selfish reasons. What does that make me? No better than the one I instructed to do so.

What have I done? I didn't raise Modir from the Valley of Death to be my assassin! But here I am—controlling her actions and telling her whom to kill for me. This wasn't how it was supposed to be. She was supposed to come back to take her rightful place as the Blodheksa and tear open the sky. And I was supposed to be by her side assisting *her*. Now, I set her off to do *my* bidding?

This isn't right.

This isn't right.

This isn't...

Chapter Seventeen

Soon enough, Arik and Modir shuffle into the cave. Quickly, I grab a blanket by the altar and rush to Modir's side to wrap her in it—to cover her naked, blood-bathed body. I pray with all my might that they didn't cross paths with Trond and Aizel on their journey home.

"No," Arik says. "It was clear."

I let out a heavy sigh. "Trond ran off, and Aizel followed. He is not handling this well."

Arik's orange eyebrows rise, and his eyes go large and round as he looks quickly to Modir at his side and back to me.

"I know," I say, acknowledging his gesture. "Has there been much of a change?"

He shakes his head and steps aside to make some space between himself and Modir—just enough room for me to slip in and examine her, but keeping an arm's-length distance in case I needed assistance. "See for yourself."

I scan her face, looking for a sign of the old Modir, looking for something more apparent than just the dimly lit spark brewing behind her eyes. Something more tangible. More hopeful. Something that screams to me that "she's back to her regular self!" But there is nothing. She tracks my facial movements, is cognizant of my presence like she was when she first awoke, but her eyes… her eyes give no indication that she recognizes or even remotely remembers me. Her face scrunches a little like she's trying to narrow her eyes, to furrow her brow, to scan the recesses of her memory to pull forth the sliver of recall that would tell her just where and how she knows me. "Her eyes are still white," I observe dejectedly. I snap my fingers in front of her face as if they catch her attention. "Modir? Modir? It's Blodwyn. Your daughter."

She opens her mouth to respond, but only a groan comes out. It's long and deep and fills the halls of the cave with its haunting sound.

Frustration comes over me, and I stamp my foot like a petulant child. "She should have been... been... *more* by now!"

Arik sighs.

"This wasn't my intention," I say as I circle around her, looking her up and down, holding her arms out and letting them drop limply back at her sides. They fall heavy with a thud against her like there is no controllable reasoning or thought. "How does she not have her reflexes back?" I murmur.

Arik sighs again.

"Nothing?" I snap at him. "You have no opinion or insight? You have nothing to say about her?"

"What do you want me to say, Blodwyn?" he says solemnly. "There are no words that I could say that you don't already know."

I stop in my tracks and turn to face her again. Gently, I come in close and smile, but it's hard to hold back the tears. It's hard to dismiss what Arik said. "You are in there," I say softly to her. "I know you are. I see glimpses of you and your pregnant belly bounding in the fields chasing after rabbits. I see images of you in the circle surrounded by smokey braziers. We can do that again, Modir. We can build more memories now." I pause, pull in closer to her ear, and whisper, "We have so much work to do. Our kin need to come home."

With a tired hand, Modir swipes woefully at my upper arm, and I conclude what I had not wanted to admit. "I don't understand why she hasn't healed," I say, bewildered. "She consumed, ate, drank. She had started to repair herself, but..."

"You drove her to go to the village," Arik finishes.

"My energy."

"Your will. Your desire. But look at her. You brought her back to life, but is she *alive*?"

I close my eyes and shake my head. The tears burn down my cheeks and sting my eyes.

This is no kind of life.

"This is an abomination," he says like a gut-punch to my stomach.

I reach out and pull her into an embrace. Underneath the iron smell of caked on blood on top of the smell of grass and the earth, she is sweet. Berries. Just like I remember. I squeeze her closer, and closer still—so close that I want to incorporate our bodies and souls into one because, maybe, if I could do that, she would really be able to stay. For seventeen years, she was mine. My Modir. My life-giver. My guide.

And then she wasn't.

And for seven years I wrestled with the emotions—that odd in-between state of acceptance and denial and sadness and anger. There's a level of disbelief when someone is ripped from this plane of existence and thrust into one where you cannot see them, or hear them, or touch them. Reality bends, and I had set out to bend it back, to make things right, to reclaim what was stolen from me.

And I did.

But only for a few hours.

I missed you, I think I hear her say to me.

"I missed you more," I say shakily through the knot in my throat.

The heat from my arms and chest soon ignites the bloodied blanket around her body. What little flesh she has attached to her bones burns with a crisping sound, and her tangled red braid singes to her scalp. For a second I think I won't let go—we'll go up in flames together. Arik swoops over and pulls me away, but I am unharmed, unfazed, unburnt. I couldn't kill myself even if I wanted to. The runes from Modir have protected me and will protect me for the rest of time.

So why couldn't they have protected her?

I rest my head on Arik's shoulder and watch as Modir's body burns and twists and turns and finally crumbles to the ground in an ashy pile.

Arik helps me sweep up the last remnants of her, and we take the ashes to her grave where we bury her properly—the way we should have done seven years ago.

Chapter Eighteen

In the Time of Darkness
In the Age of Ice
Summertime, 673 AD
Caverns in the Far North
Afternoon of the Half Moon

I t is done. Modir's ashes have been returned to the ground where she can continue to nourish the earth with her powerful essence. Now I know that's what I should have done all along. Everyone was right—Grom, Aizel, Sorcia—all of them had advised against burying her body or had at least communicated their apprehension to me. I had been wrong. I know that now—I see that now. And it kills me inside to admit my wrongdoings.

"You weren't wrong," Arik says as we walk back to the cave. "You did what you thought was right."

I stop in my tracks and turn to face him. "You never once doubted me," I say and kiss him gently on the cheek. "All these years together. All this time. You never wavered even though you knew I would fail."

"I didn't know."

I narrow my eyes. "You had a feeling I would fail."

"But did you fail? Did you really fail? You accomplished what you set out to do; it just had a different outcome from what you planned."

"But in doing so, I lost my purpose. Now, I'm back at the beginning. With Modir really gone—gone for good—where does that leave me? Who am I? What role do I have to play in bringing back the old ones?"

He pulls me into his chest, presses his lips on the top of my head, and smothers me with gentle fluttery kisses. I melt into him as if each peck is a sign of validation. *Everything is going to be fine. We will figure this out together.*

I slip my arm around his back, and we walk together side by side. The summer sun of midday beats down on us, and I close my eyes and lift my face to the sky letting the warmth soak into me. The world glows orange behind my lids as black speckles move back and forth across my vision. The world will look like this for real when I restore the ancients back to their rightful place. Their power and glory will scorch the earth and leave us with a permanent smoldering landscape. I can almost smell it now—like the way Modir's flesh singed within my embrace. I breathe in deep, let the crisp air fill me with all its aromatic goodness, and exhale with a satisfying sigh as I envision the future. My future. Our future. With Arik, and Aizel, and Trond by my side, I am eager to regroup and restart our true mission.

But my hopeful dreams are dashed when we arrive at the cave and the heightened voices from inside get closer and closer within earshot. Desperate tones dance off the rock walls. Pleading sounds fill the halls. Frantic voices rumble and rattle in the hearth. And familiar sobs strike my heart deep.

Trond.

Trond is crying.

Trond is in trouble.

Quickly, I race to the vestibule, and my jaw nearly drops at the sight that waits for me. Sorcia holds Trond from behind with her ceremonial blade pressed against the side of his neck. Her face is streaked with dirt and blood, and her clothes are tattered — as if something, or someone, had attempted to ravage her, or kill her. Like Evanak emerging from her cave all those eons ago, I wonder how Sorcia managed to escape the wrath of Modir in the town that she decimated. Tears stream down Trond's face as he tries hard to control his sobs. Aizel stands a few feet away from them, arms stretched out in front of her so as to calm Sorcia down. Aizel speaks softly, gently, but Sorcia's booming voice fills the cavern with an ominous rage.

"You!" Sorcia screams when she sees me, and she points the blade in my direction. Her eyes are wild and filled with a blackness I have never seen from her before, like she has been completely consumed with a draugr of pure hate.

Frantically, I look to Arik, my eyes pleading for his help. He takes a step forward, but Sorcia puts the knife back on Trond and presses down. A thin line of red slides down the side of his neck and he squirms and tries to stifle a squeal. "Stay where you are!" Sorcia commands Arik, and he abides.

"What are you doing? What is all this?" I try saying calmly.

"You," she growls in a low and guttural voice. "You were supposed to be my sister." She digs the blade a little harder into Trond. "We were supposed to always be there for each other. Support each other. And what do you do? You do nothing but destroy. You're a destroyer, Blodwyn. You don't care about anyone but yourself."

I put up my hands defensively to show her I am not carrying a weapon, and I take a step forward. "Sorcia, let Trond go. Your issue is with me. He has nothing to do with it. He's just a little boy. A little innocent boy. Let him go, and let's talk this out. You and me."

"There's not much time for talking, Blodwyn," Aizel calls over loudly.

I keep my eyes trained on Sorcia, but call back from the side of my mouth, "What does that mean?"

Trond flinches again and lets out a small cry.

"Ruz! Ruz! Look at me. Look at me. I'm right here. Don't worry. I'll keep you safe," I try to coax.

He fidgets, and Sorcia tightens her grip to force him to stop squirming.

"She poisoned him," Aizel says, her voice strong and unwavering.

Keeping my gaze on Trond and Sorcia, I tilt my head in her direction, trying to process her words. *Sorcia? Poisoned Trond? What is she talking about?*

Look! I hear a voice call from beyond, and all at once the world stops, and my heart stops, and my brain stops, and I feel as if I can't catch my breath.

"Blodwyn! Did you hear me?" Aizel calls out again. "Sorcia found Trond in the woods before I did and set a snake on him."

Trond's arm dangles pitifully at his side. The skin at the crook of his palm, where his thumb meets his forefinger, is almost completely black, and the discoloration from dark purple to violet to green to yellow is already creeping up the length of his arm. I want to rush over to them, snatch him from her clutches, and slam her head against the rock wall so her brain spills out at my feet, but I can't. I'm paralyzed. Frozen. I want to scream, but nothing comes out. My mind can't even come up with a charm to cease the progression of the venom in Trond's veins.

"Don't even think about it. Don't even try to get him from me, and don't even try to get into my head," Sorcia spits. "You took away the one thing I truly loved. Now, by venom or by blade, I will take away what is most precious to *you*! I can cut him right and make it fast, or we can wait it out and let the poison reach his heart. Either way, you're going to watch Trond die."

Ruz! I call to him directly. *Breathe slowly. Be not afraid. I go before you, always. If you panic, it will make it worse. Try to relax. Keep your good thoughts flowing...*

His gray eyes go wide, and he nods to me.

"Tricky, tricky," Sorcia sings clicking her tongue against the roof of her mouth. "Talk to him all you like, Blodwyn. Might as well get it all out while you can."

"Why, Sorcia?" I plead. "It didn't have to be this way."

"You're right. It didn't have to be this way. But it always was with you. You made it be this way. Your dreams and your power and your quest for glory."

"Trust me, there was no such thing," I huff.

"You might have Aizel fooled, you might have your manservant fooled, you might even have yourself fooled, but make no mistake, Blodwyn, you only wanted to raise your mother from the dead just so you can say you did it. It's as simple as that. It was just so you could say you did something great and wonderous. Something that set you off as better than the rest of us. Because you always saw yourself as better than us. Always."

Sorcia presses the blade against Trond's neck again, and Aizel gasps uncontrollably. "Breathe, Trond!" she instructs him. "Slow and steady."

"Why, Aizel, so the boy can last 'til sundown? Why make him prolong the process?"

Aizel opens her mouth to respond, but I raise my hand to silence her.

Sorcia laughs. "Exactly what I mean. Blodwyn commands, and everyone obeys! I was so blind! Blind to the manipulations of a power-hungry crazy person."

Suddenly, it dawns on me—if I had the ability to give sight to Arik, I must also have the ability to take sight away.

"Sorcia!" I scream.

She jolts at attention, startled, and I am able to lock eyes with her. I hold her gaze in mine with a lulling stare, and I fall into their blackness, their darkness, and tumble down into the depths of her *fylgja*—her soul, her essence, her core. She fights hard, trying to resist my mental invasion, but I sing songs from our childhood and lilt my inner voice to a sweet and gentle timbre that makes it hard for her to resist me.

Oh, sweet Sorcia. Sweet sister. Why didn't you ever tell me of your fears? Your doubts? Your apprehensions? You let all your insecurities build up inside you for far too long. We could have resolved all of this ages ago had you just opened your heart to me. But there's still time, my sweet, sweet sister. We can repair the damage we have caused to one another.

My voice in her mind soothes her, and she drops the knife at Trond's neck to the ground. Having the upper hand, I send images of our childhood to her mind—happy memories of us and Aizel, and Modir, and the cave, and the hunt, and our circle—all the tasty morsels of what made

233

our time together innocent and fun and carefree. A little smile forms at her mouth, and she sways for a second, indulging in the feeling, getting lost in those thoughts. In her head, she stays there for what feels like years reliving the best moments of her life—dancing and playing under the gnarled winter trees of the Frostheim, calling the corners with Aizel and me, and conjuring the most basic of spells. Within seconds, though, I feel her push and pull on the inside, fighting me off and clawing her way back to reality. When she manages to come back into her own consciousness, I am ready and waiting to pounce. Rapidly she blinks her eyes to regain her focus and escape my psychic hold, but she panics when she realizes there is no focus to be had! With all the strength I can summon, I snuff out her vision like blowing out a torch in the cave.

When the realization sets in that she has opened her eyes up to darkness, she frantically flails her arms and flings Trond to the side of the vestibule. Aizel races over and cradles him to help maintain his composure. She knows just as well as I do that every fluttering heartbeat in his chest only spreads the venom quicker throughout his body.

"What have you done to me?" Sorcia howls and spins herself wildly around and swats her arms blindly in the air as if to reach for me. "I'll kill you! I'll kill you both! I'll kill you all! You're a destroyer, Blodwyn! A destroyer! God will punish you for all your sins! For all your..."

Chapter Eighteen

Without saying a word, Arik creeps up behind her. She senses his presence, and for a moment, she stops moving.

"It didn't have to be like this, Sorcia," I say one last time before Arik crosses his hands around her head gripping each side of her face and forcefully twists them in opposite directions. A loud *snap* fills the room, and Sorcia crumples to the rock floor with a *thud*.

At the exact same moment, as if connected to her curse, Trond goes limp in Aizel's arms. "Blodwyn!" she shrieks, her voice cutting through every inch of the cave.

I waste no time and turn to them. Trond's arm has gone completely black from wrist to bicep, and his face is saturated with fever-sweat. "Trond," I say, gently shaking him.

His body jerks forward and languidly back against Aizel's chest.

"Trond?" I say louder, shaking him more forcefully. "Ruz! Wake up! Sorcia's gone now. Aizel and I are going to fix you."

But he doesn't move. Aizel's face is overcome with fear—fear and sadness—for we've been down this road before.

"He's dying?" I cry, my voice crackly and pained.

Aizel lowers her head, unable to meet my gaze straight on, and nods.

"Does he know he's dying?" I ask. This scene feels hauntingly familiar as if she and I have had this conversation before.

Aizel looks down, puts her palms over Trond's face, and closes her eyes. She fishes through his mind, trying to pull out his active thoughts. "I can't tell. I think he has some notion. He's in a dream right now, I think. But it's not really a dream. There are colors and lights and sounds, but nothing..." she pauses and crinkles her nose, "nothing ... *tangible*."

"The venom has already reached his brain," I say matter-of-factly.

She opens her eyes with a pained expression and nods again.

Quickly, I jump to my feet, "We have to act fast!" I say. "I'll draw the circle, and..."

Aizel reaches up and grabs my wrist. "There's no time, Blodwyn," she says sorrowfully and drags me back to the ground with them. "There's no time."

Her touch is like ice against my fiery skin. A thousand snowflakes against a thousand embers. And in my frantic state of mind, there is no room for thought, no room for error. Music from the forest fills my head with epic songs of our ancient kin. Modir sings again—her voice like a bell from beyond. She lets me know she is at peace, and she lets me know that through me, with me, and in me, in the unity of the heksas of time, all glory and honor is mine, forever and ever.

Mine.
Forever.

Modir tells me that is how long I will reign—forever in many forms, in many lifetimes, in many different capacities.

"Blodwyn. Blodwyn!" Aizel says, but her voice is far away. I can't answer her now. There is so much more I need to learn, and there is very little time left. Modir sings me a song called the *Aevir*. Eternal. For that is what I am, and that is the gift I bestow.

Forever.

The den of snakes encircle us, and Arik stands outside of them keeping watch. They bless us with their presence and protection. They give me their eyes to see through, and for the first time, I see the wonderous prismatic colors of the world—colors that have no name to the human tongue, colors that represent emotions and thoughts and temperature.

Heat.

I look down at my arms and chest, and I am lit up like the summer sky. My snake eyes show me how my body glows and surges with warmth and light. They burn so hot, that I'm afraid I will incinerate like Modir. *But you won't*, she sings to me. *That is your gift. Be not afraid.*

Without hesitation, I grip Aizel's wrist with my right hand and Trond's wrist with my left. She gasps and makes a croaking sound in her throat when I begin the flow of my energy into them. I let go—every ounce of me, every black tattooed brand on my flesh dissipates into my veins and streams into them. I release it all until my markings have faded from my flesh and a chill settles into my spine.

Aizel closes her eyes and smiles a closed-mouth smile. My energy is warm like a pleasure swell between her legs. Her face starts to glow with life. Trond's arm is no longer blackened with venom.

When the transfer of power is complete, the snakes slither away and Aizel's eyes open, like she was awakened from a dream that felt all too real. "Blodwyn?" she whispers.

I give a small smile. "It wasn't a dream," I mutter, but I am weak, and I can feel death all around me. Inside me. The venom from Trond's veins blackens my insides, hollows me out.

I'm dying.

My vision gets blurry and dim. No longer can I see with the bright light colors of the snakes. And with my vision fading, it's only a matter of time before Arik's fades as well.

Aizel's eyes widen when the reality of my demise sets in. "What did you do?" she asks, but she knows the answer already.

"You are like me now," I answer.

She reaches for my hand. "Oh, Blodwyn, you're so cold! And you're no longer marked! What happened? What have you done?"

I nod my head at Trond. His chest puffs up in his wonder-filled dream, and I smile. "He's better now. And he will live for a long, long while. Like you."

Tears spring to her eyes. "Oh, no! No!" she cries. "I can't lose you! We have so much more to do together."

Arik kneels at my side, I wrap my arm around his neck, and he lifts me up. "You need to do those things with Trond now. He will grow just enough to be of age, then you both will have each other to hold on to and finish what we started. The books, Aizel. You need to finish them. Once you two have done what needs to be done, you will be free of your mortal coils and open to the flames. Be wary of the flames, Aizel. You cannot create them, but in your end, they will dance in your eyes."

"I don't know what that means!" she cries desperately. "Blodwyn, I promise you, I'll bring you back. I'll bring you back like you brought back Modir!"

"No, Aizel. Not like that. I should have never buried her. I should have never brought her back. Arik will put me on the pyre, and he will leave my ashes at Modir's gravesite. If you must do it, find another way. Modir was an abomination, and what I did was unforgivable. Find another way. I don't want to be like that."

"Will you come back to us?" she asks Arik.

Arik shakes his head and repositions me in his arms.

"Once Blodwyn is gone, I will be back in darkness," he says solemnly.

"I've taken the memory of Arik away from Trond," I say. "I fear it would be too much for him to take."

Aizel strokes Trond's hair back from his forehead, her tears streaming onto his cheeks. "What do I tell him? What do I say?"

I open my mouth to speak, but a chilling wave swells in my chest and paralyzes my vocal chords. The words are frozen in my throat. I look to Arik, panicked, but he kisses me deep, taking the words off the tip of my tongue. He too has tears at the sides of his eyes, and I can tell he is fighting hard to prevent them from spilling over.

It was always you, I say to his mind, and he no longer can control their release.

"Blodwyn says to tell Trond she's sorry," Arik replies to Aizel. I close my eyes and rest my head against his shoulder listening to him speak my words for me. His voice is comforting, and I am at peace knowing he can relay to Aizel what's in my heart. "She says she's sorry she couldn't stay with you both. She's sorry she couldn't open the sky and rain blood upon this world. She's sorry for all the pain she's brought upon you. She has a different path now, but she will see you again. Aizel, my sweet sister. *You* are the Blodheksa. It will be you. This I know. Ruz, keep your good thoughts flowing and your actions to match."

Arik makes his way out of the cave and back into the forest to take me to my final spot. I rest my chin atop his shoulder and open my eyes just enough to see Trond stirring awake in Aizel's arms. She smothers his face in a thousand kisses and shrieks out in happiness that he is well.

In the corner of the cave, my snakes bow their heads in reverence to me as a final goodbye. As we move farther out of the cave, their bodies commingle into a white blur. They are hazy in my weakening vision and appear to take the shape of one giant snake. Further still, the giant snake body twists and turns and morphs into the shape of a woman lying on the rock floor, white hair strewn across the jagged granite. I smile again because I know I will be there. Always. In that cave, with Aizel and Trond.

For I am one with the White Serpent.

I am the White Serpent.

I am the Witch of the White Serpent.

Book Club Questions

1. How would you describe the role of love in this novel?

2. How does the loss of Blodwyn's mother impact both her humanity and her role as a witch?

3. What, if any, significance is there to the lack of a father figure in Blodwyn and Trond's lives?

4. Do you think Blodwyn was right that Sorcia was jealous of her? Or was Sorcia right and Blodwyn is a destroyer?

5. Many say that Christianity and witchcraft are at odds with each other. Here we see elements of Christianity. Discuss.

6. What role does double-vision hold in the novel?

7. Discuss the importance of the number 3 in the novel.

8. How do you feel about the origin story of the ancients?

9. "One of man's greatest downfalls is his avarice and his quest for power." Blodwyn shows this to Michael in the story of the ancients. Discuss the relevance of this quote within the greater context of the novel.

10. As the novel progresses, we see Blodwyn assuming her ultimate form. She openly compares herself to Jesus, but she also bares similarities to Michael and the Devil. Who do you think she's the most similar to and why?

11. Change is a central theme to the novel. Which change(s) struck you most?

12. What does the phrase "no child should be without its mother" mean to you?

13. Why snakes? Would Blodwyn be somehow different if a different animal came to her?

14. Our childhoods shape us. Did Trond witnessing Modir's rampage shape him into something sinister? Or was Aizel right and he was always going to be that way?

Author Bio

Maria DeVivo writes horror and dark fantasy for both a YA and an adult audience. Each of her series has been Amazon best-sellers and have won multiple awards since 2012. When not writing, she teaches Language Arts and Journalism to middle school students in Florida. A lover of all things dark and demented, the worlds she creates are fantastical and immersive. Get swept away in the lands of elves, zombies, angels, demons, and witches (but not all in the same place). Maria takes great pleasure in warping the comfort factor in her readers' minds—just when you think you've reached a safe space in her stories, she snaps you back into her twisted reality.

PAIGE LAVOIE
I'm in Love with Mothman

ROBERT J. LEWIS
Shadow Guardian and the
Three Bears

T.S. SIMONS
Antipodes
The Liminal Space
Ouroboros
Caim
Sessrúmnir
The 45th Parallel

VALERIE WILLIS
Cedric: The
Demonic Knight
Romasanta: Father of
Werewolves
The Oracle: Keeper of the
Gaea's Gate
Artemis: Eye of Gaea
King Incubus:
A New Reign

V.C. WILLIS
The Prince's Priest
The Priest's Assassin
The Assassin's Saint

HORROR, THRILLER, & SUSPENSE

ALAN BERKSHIRE
Jungle
Hell's Road

ERIKA LANCE
Jimmy
Illusions of Happiness
No Place for Happiness
I Hunt You

STEVE ALTIER
The Ghost Hunter

MARIA DEVIVO
Witch of the Black Circle
Witch of the Red Thorn
Witch of the Silver Locust

MARK TARRANT
The Mighty Hook
The Death Riders
Howl of the Windigo
Guts and Garter Belts

**DISCOVER MORE AT
4HorsemenPublications.com**